Dog-Nabbed

Susan J. Kroupa

LAUREL FORK PRESS

Books by Susan J. Kroupa

The Doodlebugged Mysteries
Bed-Bugged
Out-Sniffed
Dog-Nabbed
Bad-Mouthed
Ruff-Housed
Mis-Chipped

A Most Magical Christmas

Published by Laurel Fork Press
Laurel Fork, Virginia
www.laurelforkpress.com

Photo and Cover Credits:
Labradoodle © 2016 by Susan J.Kroupa
Cover Design © by Susan J. Kroupa
Book Design © by Marny K. Parkin

For all the lost dogs the world over,
And for all those who help them find
food, warmth, and family

Contents

Chapter 1

Marmie's and Grandjum's

"DAD, DOODLE THREW UP." MOLLY HALF TURNS IN her seat.

It's true. For some time now, the boss has been driving over a road that curves this way and that, not to mention goes up and down a lot. I was having a great time, enjoying the view and all the scents—if I'm sitting or standing, I'm tall enough to see out of the windows of the van from my crate, which is really a type of wire cage, not the solid plastic kind that I have for inside the house—but then I got tired and curled down for a nap. And suddenly my stomach just felt awful. And up came the treats that Molly gave me at the last rest stop, plus the good-sized chunk of hamburger she slipped me at lunch when the boss wasn't looking.

"Great. That's just what we need," the boss says, sounding more upset than the situation calls for. We dogs don't worry much about vomit and most of the time clean it up ourselves by re-eating it. Humans think that's disgusting, but dogs don't like to waste food, and, to be honest, it tastes as good to us the second time around.

So I plan to take care of it when the van quits swaying from side to side and my stomach settles a bit.

But the van slows down, and then stops. The boss hops out and pulls open the side door. "Where are those wipes?" he asks, as he clips on my leash and opens the door to my crate.

I guess we're taking another break. Now that we're stopped, the puddle of food looks better to me and I quickly polish it off.

"Euwww." Molly takes the leash and leads me to the side of the road.

Like I said, humans don't get the concept.

The boss takes out his cell phone. "Hey, we finally have a signal!" He punches a key on his phone. "Dad?"

I hear a man's voice come through the phone—dogs have excellent hearing compared to humans—but I'm more interested in the wonderful bouquet of scents on a tall sprig of grass. At least two different dogs, traces of deer, and beneath it all a faint hint of mouse. Is this a great day or what?

"We're running late," the boss says. "So go ahead with lunch, and we'll grab a bite when we get there." He listens for a bit while I sort out all sorts of fascinating scents, and then says, "Okay. But if you get hungry, go on ahead. No telling if we'll have to stop again with Doodle."

Hey. Didn't I clean it up? And I feel a lot better now that I'm out in the fresh air.

"Doodle, don't pull!" Molly says, holding up her camera with her free hand. She snaps some photos while I sniff—each of us doing what we love best.

After a bit, Molly puts away her camera and pulls out her phone, and soon I hear Tanya's voice.

Tanya Franklin, Molly's very best friend, goes to the same school as Molly, where they learn all sorts of stuff about science and also Spanish, which I understand a little of myself. (Spanish, not science.) Just thinking about Tanya—or any of the Franklins for that matter—makes me happy. They're my favorite family, next to Molly and the boss, of course.

Molly tells her that I got carsick—not sure why everyone's making such a big deal of this—while I add a few more of my marks to a nice assortment of bushes.

"We're about forty-five minutes from Marmie and Grandjum's," Molly says.

"Grandjum?" Tanya giggles at the name.

"It's for Grandpa Jim. When I was little that's how I said it, and it kind of stuck."

Molly promises to call Tanya when we get to her grandparents. She punches a few keys and I hear that whirring sound that phones make when people call. And then a man's voice says, "You have reached the Combs' residence. Please leave a message."

Molly frowns, leading me back to the van. "She never answers."

The boss opens the door and shuts me into my crate. "Who?"

"Lizzie." Molly clicks her phone shut. "I've been trying for weeks."

Lizzie is Molly's other best friend, according to what I've heard Molly tell Tanya. I've never met her. She lives in the Blue Ridge Mountains near where the boss went to high school, which is where we're going now, to visit Molly's grandparents. Molly hasn't seen her friend since she and the boss moved to

Arlington—not sure how long ago, but before the boss got me to be part of his bed-bug detecting business.

"We can drop by while we're here," the boss says.

"Yeah. But it's weird that she doesn't answer."

Pretty soon we're on the road again. I settle down for a nap and the next thing I know the van is turning and I hear the squeaky crunch of tires on gravel.

Molly already has the window down and her camera clicking as we pull up. I sit up and peer out the van window at a long, single-story house that sits on a hill under the branches of two massive trees.

Now this is what I call a yard! A broad area of grass surrounded by trees and flower beds. Brown right now, of course, since it's that time of year, although everyone keeps saying it's unusually mild for November—not sure what they mean by that. A field on one side of the house, and woods on the other. Not a fence in sight, or a neighboring house for that matter.

A dog could really enjoy himself here. Plenty of room to do what humans like to call "our business" without leaving any of the scent near the house. Our yard in Arlington is a small one, although Molly and the boss keep it pretty clean. Still, the scent always lingers, at least for dogs. Humans are pretty much blind to scents, if you catch my drift.

"Well, here we are," the boss says. As soon as he opens the car door, I know that a dog lives here. Sure enough, when the door opens and a man and woman hurry out to greet us, they're accompanied by an older hound. He barks a couple of times just to let us know it's his place. I don't answer. No need to be disrespectful.

"Hey, Marmie. Hey, Grandjum." Molly jumps out to hug first a plump woman with short gray hair and lively dark eyes, and then a man who looks a lot like the boss, only older, thinner, and without the boss's beard. "We brought Doodle."

Speaking of which, I'm still in my crate. I stand and press my nose against the wire, looking alert, hoping that the boss will let me out. But now he's busy hugging the couple. "Hey, Mom, Dad. So good to see you." I give a one-bark reminder, which serves its purpose as everyone turns to look at me.

Marmie smiles. "He's some dog, from what I hear."

"That he is," the boss says in a tone that implies it's not a great thing. Always a bit hard to please, the boss is, although at heart he's a gentle man and never mean.

Molly reaches through the crate and attaches the leash. Just because once I sort of bolted and ran away as Molly was getting me out of the crate, the boss has this rule that the leash has to be clipped on before the gate is opened. He never forgets anything.

I hop out and greet the hound stiffly, until we're both assured that neither one of us is going to be aggressive. "Doodle, this is Bridger," Molly says. "He's a Walker hound."

Then Molly takes me over to meet her grandparents.

Grandjum gives me a few pats on the head, which I don't particularly like but endure politely. "So this is the world famous bed-bug slayer."

Slayer? My job is to find the bugs. I leave it to others to get rid of them, although I have on occasion eaten a few. Molly's grandfather smells like wood smoke, car oil, coffee, and Bridger. He's dressed in loose jeans and a flannel shirt, much like the boss himself.

"Look at this clear air," the boss says, taking a few deep breaths. "Wish we could make a go of it here."

Ever since I've known the boss, which has been for some time, although I'm not exactly clear how long, he's wished he could move back to the Blue Ridge Mountains. According to him, when his folks left the deserts of Arizona—never been there myself—to move to Laurel Woods, he felt as if he'd entered an enchanted forest. "In a good way," he always adds.

I have to say, as I take in the crisp air, fragrant with leaf mold, trees, grass, and animals, I agree with him. I'd live here in a heartbeat.

"Hey, Sweetie." Marmie bends over and scratches me under the chin, something I really like. She's also dressed in jeans and flannel—must be a family thing. And she smells much the same, too, except for a delicious smell of cooking meat—pot roast, I think—on her clothing, and the scent of raw onions on her hands.

"I think you and Bridger are going to have some fine times together." She scratches some more and then, with some effort, straightens up.

"Grandjum fixed up your dad's old bike," she says to Molly. "Oh and—" She turns to the boss. "Stu called and said that if you still want to come over, tonight would be good. Louisa's feeling up to company. He tried to get you on your cell."

The boss checks his phone. "Hey, I got a signal here. Hardly had one for the whole trip. Yeah, I see he left a message." He lifts a suitcase down from the back of the van.

Grandjum smiles. "That's why we keep a landline. Although our cells probably work better than yours. Who's your carrier?"

I don't hear the answer because Bridger and I do some more sniffing. But then Marmie says something that catches my attention.

"—pot roast."

Already smelled it, of course, and I'm glad to hear it's for dinner, but the boss's face spreads into a smile. "Pot roast?"

Marmie laughs. "I know my boy," she says. But then she shakes her head. "I planned dinner early so you'll have plenty of time before you go over to see Louisa." She sighs. "Poor Louisa. I don't think she has long left. And with Will being such a jerk…"

The boss sets down a case and glances up in surprise. "Will?"

Molly goes still, her eyes intent on Marmie.

"Hadn't you heard? Zeke—that's his uncle on his father's side—got hold of him. Zeke thinks he's some kind of prophet who speaks for God." Marmie shakes her head. "And he believes you shouldn't associate with non-believers, so Louisa can't see Nettie or her granddaughters. I'm sure she'll tell you all about it. Oh—and that reminds me." She reaches into the pocket of her jacket and pulls out a letter that she holds out to Molly. "This came for you the other day. From Lizzie."

Wide-eyed, Molly takes the letter and turns it over. It has writing in big black letters. The boss leans over her shoulder and reads out loud, "MRS. HUNTER, WILL YOU PLEASE GIVE IT TO MOLLY? IT'S IMPORTANT." He smiles. "I could see Lizzie writing that. She's always been a firebrand."

Not sure what he means. Molly tears open the envelope, moving away from the others a little, like a dog with a bone she doesn't want to share, and pulls out a piece of paper, scanning it quickly. She folds it and starts to put it away, and then notices the boss, Grandjum, and Marmie all staring at her.

"What's it say?" Marmie asks.

Molly bites her lip a little and stiffens slightly, but then unfolds the paper and reads out loud,

Hey, Molly,

I hope you get this.

I seen you called and emailed and left a gazillion messages but I can't answer 'cause of Uncle Zeke. He's my daddy's uncle, so I guess he's really my great uncle or something. Anyways, Daddy won't let us see no one unless Uncle Zeke approves, because Daddy thinks he speaks for God and anything he says goes. I don't see it myself unless God is boring and a little mean and don't care for folks much, because that's how UZ is. That's what I call him. Ooo-zeee like the rifle. We're supposed to call him Mr. Combs or Uncle Zeke, but I call him UZ cause he's like that rifle in the hands of a crazy person shooting down everything good. Not to his face, of course.

So that's why I don't answer your emails. Mama now checks every email I send, just another reason I WISH I had my own computer and cell phone. Back before UZ, Daddy talked about letting me earn money for my own phone. But now, Mr. Holy Man Zeke proclaims cell phones are worldly and no one should really have them, especially kids. If I'm ever alone in the house, which ain't likely 'cause Mama stays home more since she can't see her friends, I'll try to sneak a call on the landline.

Here's the important part. If you get a chance to see Mamaw, tell her and Papaw me and Becca miss them terribly and if UZ wasn't here we'd be over there all the time. Mama don't talk much about missing them but I know she does and sometimes when she goes down for a nap, I hear her crying. I don't know why she don't just tell UZ to butt out. When I asked her once, she told me scripture says it's the wife's duty to follow her husband and that Daddy has enough on his mind without her causing problems and don't say no more about it. I don't understand that, 'cause Mama's always been strong and done what she likes no matter what Daddy says, but when Adam died she changed and kind of sunk into herself. And UZ's always putting her down if she says so much as a word.

So, anyway, I wish I could see you but it'd likely take a miracle with UZ stuck to us like a tick on a dog.

I'm sneaking this to the mail and hope your grandma gives it to you.

I miss you.

> Love,
> Lizzie

For a moment, no one speaks. Molly stares at the letter, frowning. Then Marmie sighs, shaking her head. "See? Just like I told you."

Chapter 2

A Different Zeke

LET'S GO INSIDE," GRANDJUM SAYS. "GETTING CHILLY out here."

No need to encourage me. We walk through a small but neat living room, with a couch and two stuffed chairs, into a spacious kitchen with white cabinets on one end, and an oval table and chairs on the other. The back wall of the kitchen has two big glass doors that open out onto a long screened-in porch.

Soon Bridger and I are stretched out on the kitchen floor while everyone else sits at the table eating pot roast. The boss and Molly tell her grandparents all about our bed-bug detecting business, how tough it was to find jobs at first, and then how there was all that drama around the certification trials.

"But things are looking up now." The boss leans back, glancing at his empty plate with a sigh of contentment. "We've got contracts with several large retirement homes and several hotels, and the list is growing." He pats his beard with his napkin and pushes his chair from the table. "Mom, I think this is the best pot roast I've ever tasted."

What? I thought Mrs. Franklin's pot roast was his favorite. At least that's what he always tells her. They smell equally good to me.

Marmie laughs. "You always did understand how to get your way with the cook through flattery. But tomorrow will be frozen pizza. I never cook big the day before Thanksgiving." She turns to Molly. "And how's that new school of yours?"

"Good," Molly says.

"All A's so far," the boss adds.

"And what are you studying?"

"It's a science school, so I have a lot of math and science and history. And Spanish."

"Ah. Spanish. That's good." Marmie picks up her plate and carries it to the sink. For some reason, a tension suddenly fills the air. "Josh says that you, um, found your mother?"

I should have guessed. There's always tension when anyone talks about Cori, Molly's mother, who left mysteriously when Molly was small. At first, everyone thought she'd gone back to Mexico to live with her family after they'd been sent back there—don't ask me for the full story because I don't really understand it all myself, but it had something to do with being illegal aliens. Not the kind in space ships that the boss watches on TV but a different kind. Anyway, it turned out that Molly's mother wasn't in Mexico after all, but working as a cop in the city next to Arlington, which is where we live. But—as I say— whenever anyone mentions her, everyone gets tense.

"Yeah." Molly's hand strays to her neck where she wears the butterfly necklace that her mother recently gave her.

Marmie gives her a sympathetic glance, then says with a strained cheerfulness, "Anyone for blackberry pie?"

Naturally, everyone says yes. After the pie, Molly feeds me

and Bridger. Only kibble, I'm sad to say, but then Marmie comes by and adds some bits of potatoes and gravy and some pieces of fat to the mix.

After that, I follow Molly into the family room, which is even bigger than the kitchen. It smells of wood and smoke, which makes sense because it has a fireplace at one end, and the walls are wood paneling, and the floor is wood also, almost the color of sand and full of little scratches and indentations. I like this wood floor much better than the shiny ones so many people have these days, although most of it is covered with braided rugs that smell like smoke and Bridger.

Grandjum is dozing in a chair by the fireplace. The boss is on the phone, arranging the visit with Louisa. I'm not really listening, but then I hear him say, "Doodle?" in a surprised voice, and I perk up my ears.

"I suppose we could bring him," he says without enthusiasm. "If she really wants to see him." He says goodbye, then gives Marmie an apologetic look. "I promised I'd let Annie know we made it." Judging by how often he calls her, the boss pretty much has to let Annie know about everything, which used to upset Molly but doesn't seem to as much anymore.

"Annie?" Marmie asks with sudden interest.

The boss shifts his weight, holding the phone out. "A ... friend. She works with Miguel—Doodle's trainer. We both had dogs in the cert—um, certification—trials, so sometimes we'd get together for practices. And she's taught Molly some dog training techniques." Now he's blushing furiously and he hurries from the room, saying, "I won't be long."

Marmie raises her eyebrows. "Annie, huh? Interesting." She turns to Molly. "Do you like her?"

Molly nods. "She nice."

Couldn't agree more. Not to mention Annie almost always has really good treats in her pockets.

True to his word, the boss doesn't take long, and soon I'm in my crate and we're off again. It's a short drive—before I've even had a chance to doze, the van slows and turns into a driveway that sits a little ways back from the road and ends in front of a brightly lit log home.

Before the boss turns off the engine, the front door opens. A short man with a slight stoop hurries out. He has thick oval glasses on wire frames and puffy red cheeks that remind me of a chipmunk. He's younger than Grandjum, but walks more stiffly. "Josh," he calls out, his cheeks dimpling into a smile.

"Hey, Stu," the boss says. As soon as he gets out of the van, the man gives him a big hug. Molly gets one after she gets me out of my crate.

"Come on in," Stu says. "So glad you could make it. Louisa's talked of nothing else all day." He smells like wood smoke and some medicinal odors I can't place. He's wearing jeans and a flannel shirt like everyone around here seems to do.

We follow him through a small covered porch into a living room not much bigger than ours in Arlington. I smell a distinct medicinal odor along with the scents of smoke and cats. An older woman, thin and wrapped in blankets, sits in a wheelchair by a woodstove across the room. She looks up eagerly. "Josh! Molly! How wonderful to see you."

"Hey, Louisa." The boss crosses over to hug her, and then Molly does the same while I stand politely by her side, concentrating on the fact that I smell cats. Two of them—although I can't see any right now. Probably hiding in that annoying way that cats have.

"And this is Doodle?" Louisa's voice sags with exhaustion. She's plainly sick—her face has an unnatural pallor and the lines around her eyes speak of pain.

She pats me on the head. Her breath also smells strong—tainted with that medicinal odor as well as a sickly quality. "Molly has told me great things about you."

Molly sits down in a straight back chair next to her, while the boss takes a seat on the couch. Pretty soon, they're all talking about old times, laughing, and having a good time. I decide the cats aren't going to come out of hiding, so I lie down and relax.

"I don't suppose you've talked to Lizzie?" Louisa asks in a hopeful tone.

Molly hesitates. "I haven't talked to her, but I..." She pulls out Lizzie's letter from her jacket pocket. "She sent this to me." She hands it to Louisa, who reads it out loud.

"Zeke," mutters Stu, saying the word like a curse.

I raise my head. We go to Zeke's Burgers all the time. Great place, and one of the few that allows dogs—in their outside seating, of course. Zeke's a big bear of a man with some kind of accent—not sure what except it's not Spanish or Chinese, the two I know best. Anyway, Zeke's a friendly guy to people and dogs alike.

The boss rubs his beard. "I only met him a couple of times. But I remember he had a reputation for not wanting to work? I was a teenager, so I didn't really notice him much."

That means this has to be a different Zeke. No one could not notice the restaurant Zeke.

Stu nods. "Class A leech. Feels like his job is to be a prophet and everyone else's job is to support him."

The boss frowns. "Well, lots of ministers are supported by their congregations…"

Stu shakes his head. "Zeke's main congregation is Will and one of Zeke's brothers down in Winston, who somehow believe that he, Ezekiel Jeremiah Combs, speaks God's truth and everyone ought to listen to him."

"And if you don't, then the true believers shouldn't waste their time conversing with you," Louisa adds. "Even if you're—" her voice breaks—"family."

Whoa. Her eyes well with tears and the room is flooded with emotion. I whine softly but then Molly rests a hand on my back and I relax.

"Mind you," Stu says in a bitter voice, "Will is still able to see *his* family—even though none of them believe in Zeke's church. Just had his parents over to dinner last week. But Nettie's totally cut off from her family and her mother is *dying* and all Will can say is that he doesn't think it's a good idea for us to come over. Makes you wonder about abuse. She's so isolated."

"Abuse!" The boss sounds genuinely shocked. "Will would never—"

"I have a hard time believing that myself," Louisa agrees. "Even as angry as I am at Will."

The boss rubs his beard, then puts his head in his hands. "It's hard to believe," he says at last. "Will was always such a level-headed guy. But I know he had it rough when Adam died." He stares at the carpet for moment. "Called me, sobbing, from the hospital when it happened. No one should have to lose a child, especially to something like drowning—something you think maybe you could have prevented even if there was nothing you could have done. Maybe he's just gone a little crazy and it'll pass with time."

"We kind of thought that, too," Stu says, "but"—he spreads his hands as he glances at Louisa—"we're running out of time."

"I know he was drinking a lot after Adam's death, too—"

"Zeke put an end to that," Stu says. "Alcohol is now the tool of the devil. In that he agrees with most of the Baptists around here. So, I suppose that's a good thing Zeke has done. We used to worry about Will's drinking."

Louisa says, "I don't know. I think I'd rather have Will drunk and Zeke out of his life. At least I'd be able to see Nettie and the kids." Her voice breaks again, and Stu rises and goes over to her. The boss stands up also.

"I'm sorry," he says. "I didn't mean to—"

"No." Louisa presses a tissue to her face, and looks up clear-eyed. "It's good to be able to talk about it. And I wouldn't have missed seeing Molly—and Doodle here—for the world."

"I'll talk to him," the boss says. "We go back far enough that maybe he'll listen to me."

Stu gives him a sad look. "Well, don't be surprised if he doesn't."

After that, everyone hugs again and we leave.

Chapter 3

At Lizzie's

THE NEXT MORNING, MARMIE AND GRANDJUM ARE UP before Molly and the boss.

Marmie feeds Bridger and me and then lets us outside. It's a beautiful day—chilly, but with the sun shining and the air brimming over with delicious scents: leaf mold, the cattle, possums, a hint of raccoon. And did I mention no fences?

Bridger leads me into the woods, showing me all sorts of interesting spots where we each leave our mark, and then down a steep hill to a creek. Is this great or what? We wade into it and lap up the delicious cold water. Then we go over and check out the cattle in the field next to the woods. We sample some of their poop, which Molly calls cow patties, and we both have a good roll in the tall, damp field grass. Best place ever! If the boss decides to move here, count me in.

When we get back, Marmie opens the door for us to come in. The boss, sitting at the table, looks up in alarm. "You let Doodle out without a leash?"

Marmie smiles. "Yes. Why?"

"He could run away. He costs almost ten thousand bucks."

Marmie goes over to me and scratches the place under my chin where I like it best. "You's a pricey thing, ain't ya?"

"It's the scent-detection training that's pricey, not the dog," the boss says. "He came from a shelter. But if something happens to him, I lose all my business."

Marmie's fingers move down to scratch my chest. She's a dog person, I can tell. "Well, I don't think he'll run away. He and Bridger have been outside for almost forty-five minutes and here he is, good as ever. Too much interesting stuff to do around here. Dogs run away when they have boring lives."

I give her fingers a lick, not something I normally do, but here's a human who gets it right for a change.

"Said like someone who lives in the country," the boss says. "Letting him loose in Arlington would be asking for him to get hit by a car. Or stolen."

Marmie shrugs and straightens up. "Probably true. But I think a dog that never gets to run free has a sad life."

Couldn't have said it better myself.

Molly comes in carrying my brush and a damp rag to wipe my face and paws. "Better," she says after she's cleaned me up. And then she loads me into my crate and we're off.

We drive down more winding roads, but before I have a chance to get sick, we're turning onto a gravel road that crosses a bridge over a fast moving creek. It leads to a two-storey house that sits just below the crest of a hill, out of sight from the road. There are several large garages to the side of the house as well as a small brick building with a sign over the door. A swing set, jungle gym, and picnic table sit on the other side, under the wide-spread branches of an enormous tree.

The boss parks near the house and turns off the engine. Whoa. Suddenly the tension is as thick as cheese and almost as fragrant. Molly opens the sliding door to the van, but doesn't take me out of my crate.

She and the boss walk up to the front door. A woman opens it. She's tall and slender with a pale complexion and red hair that curls down past her shoulders. Her face breaks into a wide smile. "Molly. Josh!" she exclaims.

"Hey, Nettie, how've you been?" The boss moves as if to give her a hug, but the smile drains from her face and she stands stiffly in the doorway.

Then a face peers around the woman's legs. A red-haired girl, about the age that kids first start school, stares up at the boss.

"Hey, Becca," he says in a warm voice. "Can't believe how you've grown." He shakes his head in amazement. "How old is she now?"

This brings a smile to Nettie's face. "Almost five. Already reading a few words."

Another girl comes racing around from the back of the house. She also has red hair, pulled into two long braids that flop when she runs.

"Molly!" she cries out.

"Lizzie!" Molly rushes over to her and they hug, talking in excited voices. The boss smiles, but Nettie keeps sending anxious glances towards the brick building.

"Is Will in the office?" the boss asks, following her gaze.

"Yeah. You could see him there," she says with some relief.

But then a door slams, and from the office, a man emerges, striding towards us.

"Will!" the boss says, his smile growing larger. He hurries over to meet the man.

But Will doesn't smile, and everything about the way he moves and carries his body signals that he's more annoyed than happy to see us. The hair on my back rises slightly. I push my nose against the wire in my crate.

Will walks up to the boss and they exchange words, the boss's voice happy and eager asking about Will's heating and air-conditioning business, Will's stiff and reserved as he answers in one-word sentences. Will stands a good head taller than the boss, big-boned, thin, with straight dark hair and dark eyes in a deeply tanned face.

"Got to show you Doodle," Molly says, leading Lizzie over to the van. "He's a labradoodle." She reaches through the bars of my crate, snaps on my leash and opens the door. I hop to the ground and take in all the scents.

Molly tugs gently on the leash to get my attention. "Doodle, this is Lizzie."

I sniff Lizzie's hand politely and she pats the top of my head. "He's so curly," she says.

"Yeah," Molly agrees. "He has the poodle coat." She tells Lizzie a little about our bed bug business and how I've sometimes sniffed out other things, like criminals, while Lizzie keeps patting and smiling.

And then Lizzie freezes, her head turned toward the driveway. "Oh, no," she whispers. "Here comes UZ."

An old pick-up bumps down Will's driveway, parking with a squeal of brakes, the engine shuddering to a stop. I heard the engine, of course, on the road, but hadn't paid attention. A fat Australian shepherd barks hysterically, paws on the rim of the truck bed. I had an Aussie friend once, when I was at Miguel's, my trainer. Sweet gal, and she had a very good nose, as most Aussies do. But, I'll be honest here, I've always been a little creeped out by their pale eyes. Same with malamutes. Don't know why.

This dog looks anything but sweet. Teeth bared, he barks and snarls, then whirls in circles, only to start barking again. He acts as if he's about to fend off a pack of intruders.

The truck door groans open, and the gravel crunches as a man steps out, as tall and thin as Will, with the same angular face, but his skin mottled and sunburned rather than tanned. Deep-set eyes and a prominent nose give his face an intense look. A mane of gray hair extends over his ears—maybe to make up for the fact that it's mostly gone on top. He has an expanse of white beard that reaches almost to his chest. He turns to the dog and says in a deep voice, "Rocky, shut up!"

"Hey, Zeke," Will says, waving at the man. Josh gives the man a nod. Zeke! Just as I suspected, not the same Zeke as the hamburger-place man.

"Shut up!" Zeke says again. Rocky ignores him. The man glowers at the dog, then walks around and attaches a rope to his collar, which he ties to the truck.

Although I've always been independent—deciding for myself whether I will or won't obey a command—it's no secret that in the canine world, some dogs like to be told what to do. (And in the human world, as well.) They like someone to be in charge, especially if they're a little fearful themselves. Rocky is that kind of dog. All that bark and bluster is from fear, which doesn't mean he can't be dangerous. Any fearful animal can bite when feeling threatened. I learned that the time I trapped a possum in the breezeway on the farm where I was raised. Had to have seven stitches after that encounter, and now I generally leave possums alone, although it's difficult because they are always trying to steal food, have a vile smell and are loathsome, pushy creatures with beady little eyes. And, unfortunately, sharp claws and teeth.

But, back to Rocky—it's clear that despite his yelling, Zeke is not Rocky's boss. If he were, Rocky would settle down.

"He's mean," Lizzie whispers. I'm not sure if she's talking about Zeke or Rocky. But then she adds, "Zeke doesn't believe it, even when I showed him where he bit me." She points to a thin white scar on her leg.

Zeke treads heavily over to where Josh and Will are standing. Over the smell of tension, which has suddenly strengthened, I catch a whiff of mint mixed with alcohol.

"You remember Josh," Will says, biting his lower lip. "We've been friends since—well, since you moved from Arizona your sophomore year, right?"

The boss nods and extends a hand. "Good to see you. I think we've met before, sometime way back when?" His voice has that fake heartiness it gets when he's nervous.

Zeke doesn't take the hand, but gives a curt nod.

Beside me, both Molly and Lizzie have gone dead still, their eyes fixed on the men.

"Josh is in town for the holiday," Will says.

"Actually, we came up mostly because of Louisa." The boss rubs his beard. "Stu tells me she probably doesn't have more than a month. I wanted to make sure Molly and I got to see her. She's been like a second mother to Molly—as well, of course, as a doting grandmother to Lizzie."

"Well, I hope you have a nice visit." Zeke's gaze shifts to the horizon, as if what the boss is saying is completely uninteresting.

The boss rubs his beard and clears his throat. "We did, last night, thank you. I was just telling Will that Louisa really aches to see Nettie and Lizzie before she … um, passes on. I know that the families have been, um, estranged, but Louisa doesn't have long, and surely this is a time to put aside differences."

Lizzie, still stiff as a rail, lets out her breath with a little gasp, and takes in another, holding it. A motion catches my eye. Nettie, standing in the doorway of the house, also has her eyes fixed on the men.

Zeke smiles—that is, his lips smile but his eyes are distinctly unfriendly. The hair rises higher on my back. "I've found that when people are focused on worldly values, they sometimes place importance on things that don't matter at all eternally."

"The point isn't whether it matters eternally," the boss responds in a steely voice. "It's about giving a dying woman a chance to say goodbye to her only daughter and to her grandchildren. And if it doesn't *matter* eternally, where's the harm?"

"Well, that's where you and I differ. If it doesn't matter eternally, it is unimportant to me—" he extends a hand to Will— "to us. It's not something we should spend time or energy on." He gives Will a smug look, and then waits as if expecting a response.

The scent of tension is everywhere now. Will looks at his wife, then Lizzie, and finally Zeke. Sighing, he squares his shoulders and turns to the boss. "Thanks for coming by," he says. "It was great to see you."

The boss doesn't move. He stares at his friend, his jaw dropping in disbelief. "That's it? You're going to deny Nettie the chance to say goodbye to her own *mother*? What kind of god could you possibly believe in who wouldn't allow that?"

Will doesn't answer, and when he does, his voice sounds as if he's enduring physical pain. "I'm afraid I have to ask you to go now," he said. "We don't have anything that would be beneficial for us to discuss."

"You're an idiot," the boss says. Whoa, now anger pours from him. The hair stiffens on my back and a growl forms in my throat. "An idiot to listen to an idiot like this ... this *leech* standing next to you. And an abusive one at that, to keep Nettie from her family."

Now Will's face darkens. He lets loose with a stream of what the boss calls "language." "You don't know anything. You don't know Nettie at all. If you think she isn't a hundred percent behind me, then you don't—" more language—"know her at all. You're the—" and even more language—"idiot. Now get the hell off my property."

The boss stares at Will for a second. Then without another word, he whirls and strides back toward the van.

"I knew he wouldn't let us," Lizzie whispers. She has tears in her eyes.

"Lizzie, go inside right now," Will commands.

Lizzie leans in to hug Molly and whispers something in her ear, which I might have caught with my excellent hearing, but the boss's motion sends Rocky into another round of frenzied barking. He hurtles himself against the rope.

Lizzie starts for the house. And then—uh-oh! Rocky snaps the rope. He half-leaps, half-falls off the truck and barrels straight for the boss. I can't let that happen. This Rocky really needs someone to put him in his place, to calm him down.

I lunge forward, wrenching the leash from Molly, which she was only loosely holding, and race to deflect Rocky before he bites the boss.

Everyone begins to shout at once, mostly my name and Rocky's, but I'm too busy to pay attention.

I catch Rocky when he's only a couple of dog lengths from the boss and give him a well-placed bite on the shoulder—a soft one, mind you. I'm just trying to keep him off the boss, not hurt him.

He whirls and charges for my throat. No doubt in my mind about his intentions or whether his bite will be soft. At this moment, Rocky wants to kill me. Fortunately, I'm quick and agile. I leap out of his reach and wait just long enough to lure him into the chase before running.

"Doodle!" Molly shouts, along with the boss. Zeke and Will yell at Rocky, pairing his name with a *lot* of language. They should know he's too far gone to listen. And I can't exactly obey because if I slow down Rocky's going to chew me up like hamburger.

So I run around the house, past the barns and sheds, past all the trucks, through the garden area, now brown with weeds, and back around the house again. I ease up occasionally so that Rocky won't give up on the chase and decide to go after the infinitely slower humans. His weight definitely hampers him. Finally, he stops, panting hard for a few moments before trotting over, head down, to Zeke, who grabs his collar.

I return to Molly and the boss, who are beside the van.

"Bad dog!" the boss exclaims. "*Bad* dog." He grabs the leash and with an unnecessary jerk pulls me into the crate, slamming the gate and locking it.

"He was just trying to keep Rocky from attacking you." Molly climbs into her seat and snaps her belt. "He was going to take a chunk out of your leg. He already bit Lizzie, and she has a scar, but Zeke claims she's making it up."

Trust Molly to get things right even as the boss gets them wrong.

He doesn't answer but gets in, slams the van door, and starts the engine. Soon we're back on the paved road. I wish he'd turn on the AC because I'm hot from all that running, and I'm panting hard. But he's not thinking about me. He taps his fingers on the steering wheel—something he does when he's upset.

My stomach drops as the van skids a little going around a curve and Molly says, "*Dad!*"

"Sorry." The van slows down. "I can't get over how he was so freakin' superior, like we were, I don't know, the unwashed or something."

"Lizzie's dad or Zeke?"

"Will. Zeke's—well, Zeke's always been a jerk. Has a reputation for mooching off anyone who'll listen to him preach. But Will—that surprised me. I mean, we've been friends forever. Talked to me for hours after Adam died. And suddenly he treats me like a stranger?"

He drives in silence for a bit.

He raps on the steering wheel some more, and then we're turning back into Molly's grandparents' place. "I'm sorry, Moll. I thought if I just talked to him, we could smooth things out, but instead I just made everything worse."

"At least I got to see Lizzie for a little while." Molly doesn't seem as upset as the boss, which surprises me given how excited she was to see her friend.

We ride the rest of the way in silence. Bridger greets us from the porch when we pull up. I'm glad to get out of the crate into the cool fall air. So, when Molly and the boss go inside, Bridger and I stay outside to take another round through the woods and the fields, just to make sure nothing has changed.

Chapter 4

Secret Meeting

THE NEXT DAY, MARMIE IS UP LONG BEFORE EVERYONE else. I hear her, of course, and when I click into the kitchen to see what's going on, I can tell that a feast is in the making. She's putting an enormous turkey into the oven. I'm not really fond of raw bird, but cooked turkey is something else entirely, and I can't help but hope that Bridger and I will get our share.

Before long, Molly and the boss join us in the kitchen.

"Happy Thanksgiving!" Marmie dusts some flour off her hands.

"Mom, you should have called me," the boss says. "I could have helped."

"Oh, there's still plenty left for you and Molly to do. Don't think you escaped that easily." She grins at him. "Eat your breakfast and I'll make assignments."

After breakfast, while Molly and the boss help Marmie, and Grandjum works in his shop next to the garage, Bridger and I go outside for another glorious tour of the property. When we return, we lie down in the deep leaves beneath the trees, breathing in all the rich earth scent.

We have a nice long nap before Molly comes outside, wearing her windbreaker and carrying a leash. "Can I take Doodle for a short walk?"

Uh-oh. There's that stringy quality to her voice that tells me she's nervous about something. The last time I heard her sound like this, we were sneaking into a school.

The boss, though, is clueless as usual. "Have you done all the things your grandmother asked you to do?"

"Yeah. Peeled all the potatoes and the sweet potatoes, made the green bean casserole, and cut up the fruit for the fruit salad. Oh. And set the table. Marmie said she doesn't need me anymore."

"Okay, but be back in a half an hour."

Molly puts Bridger inside so he won't follow us—not sure why he isn't welcome to come along—and we start down the driveway. I wonder if we're going to break into a school. As far as I know, there isn't one anywhere near.

As soon as we're over the first little hill and out of sight, Molly starts to run. "Hurry, Doodle." No need to tell me twice. I could easily go much faster, of course, having four legs instead of two, but I trot along beside Molly as I've been trained to do.

The driveway ends at a paved road, narrow compared to the ones in Arlington, and without a line in the middle. We run down it a short way, going around several curves until we come to a flat bridge over a busy creek. I'd like to wade in and get a drink, but Molly says, "This way," and leads me to a path that leaves the road to more or less follow the creek—up a hill, then down, and then up again and down, our feet crunching over the leaves on the ground.

Once, Molly gets her jacket caught on some blackberry thorns, and we stop while she works them loose. I know about blackberry brambles from my puppy days. Easy to get them stuck in your tail or on a leg.

We come to a spot where the trail turns and goes down a steep hill. At the bottom is a clearing where the creek widens to a little pool. Several massive trees, leafless now, of course, rise above the water.

Molly heads straight for one of the trees and rests a hand on the trunk. "Lizzie?" she calls out, but softly as if afraid she'll be overheard. When no one answers, she moves to the back of the tree. Hey, it has an opening big enough to climb into. I sniff it. Raccoons have been here, and a mouse. I sniff some more.

Molly is searching, too. "No note," she says, after a bit. She leads me back to the water and I finally get to wade in, lapping as I go. Love stream water. Best drink in the world.

Molly checks her phone, then scans the horizon as if looking for something. And then I hear footsteps. Coming from the hill opposite us.

"Doodle, hush," Molly says. Oh. Guess I was growling. Still, it's my job to keep her informed about potential intruders.

But then I catch the scent and the hair on my back settles down. It's Lizzie!

She emerges from the cluster of laurels, hurrying down the hill to the pool.

"You made it!" Molly says happily.

Molly and Lizzie hug and soon they're talking what the boss would call a mile a minute—which evidently is really fast. Just like when Molly is with Tanya Franklin, her best friend at home.

I'm not really listening because I smell a mouse under a clump of dead grass, and then there's the scent of wild turkey. Which reminds me of the turkey we're going to have for dinner.

Speaking of which, I hear Molly say, "I have to get back before long. Our dinner's at four."

"At least y'all will get one," Lizzie says. "UZ says Christmas and Thanksgiving are man-made holidays, not godly ones, so we cain't do nothing for them."

"No Christmas!" Molly's eyes brim with sympathy. "Kind of mean."

"Real mean," Lizzie agrees. "Likes to boss us around like it's his place instead of ours. And he's over all the time. He lost his wife—she up and left years back 'cause of all this prophet stuff, so he just hangs out at our place like a fly stuck on flypaper." Lizzie's mouth tightens. "I *hate* it. I wish we could go back to the way it used to be."

"Are you okay? I mean Zeke, or, um, your dad—they don't hit you or anything? Marmie said some people were worried that…" Molly skews up her face and then bites a lip… "that maybe they were, um, hurting you kids."

Lizzie looks shocked. "No. Zeke spanks a little hard, but mostly he just yells at us. And preaches. Oh, how that man loves to hear his voice—he can talk *forever*—and all of us has to pretend we's listening and honestly, it's the most boring stuff ever."

I hear something and tilt my head to listen. Footsteps again.

And then a voice comes from further up the stream. "Lizzie? Is that you?"

"UZ." The color drains from Lizzie's face. "If he sees me with you—"

Molly moves so quickly she takes me by surprise. With a little yank of the leash, she runs to the huge old tree. "Hop in," she whispers, pointing to the opening. It's a small space—not much bigger than my crate, and I'm a little reluctant, but she says, "hurry," and so I jump in. She climbs in after me. "Hush," she mouths so quietly that I hardly hear it, even with my excellent ears.

It's a tight fit. I'm crouched in the back and Molly's jammed into my side.

"Lizzie, is that you?" comes the voice again.

"Uncle Zeke," she says.

I can't see him from my position, but Zeke's scent reminds me of my second boss—the one I don't like to remember—after he'd spent an evening with his "friend" Jack Daniels.

"What're you doing here?" he demands.

"Just takin' a walk," I can hear the fear in Lizzie's voice. "It's a pretty day."

"These woods is private property," Zeke says. "My cousin owns them and he don't like no trespassers." His voice softens a tiny bit. "Even folks we know, understand?"

"But we've come here for years," Lizzie says. "Had picnics and such."

"That was okay when he didn't live up here on the mountain. But now he's back, he don't want no one on his land. Understand?"

"I guess," Lizzie says in a small voice, not sounding like she understands at all.

"And what would your daddy say if he caught you by water without any adults around? You want to be another Adam?"

"No," Lizzie mumbles.

Molly elbows me in the ribs as she switches position.

"So you run on home now, and tell your daddy that I'll be along for supper."

"Okay," Lizzie says.

"What'd you say young lady?" Zeke asks sharply.

"Yes, *sir*," she answers.

"That's better. Run along now."

Lizzie says, "Yes sir," again, and then "See you later" in a louder tone that I think was meant for Molly and me.

"Bye now," Zeke says.

We sit crammed into the hollow as still as a cat stalking a mouse until the sound from Lizzie's light footsteps and Zeke's heavier ones fade.

Molly climbs out, stretching one arm and then another. I hop out and stretch too. Did I mention it was a tight fit?

But then, I hear voices. I raise my ears, alert. Zeke's and another man.

"Everything all right?" the new man says.

Molly must hear them too (you can never tell with humans). She goes rigid and jumps back into the tree hollow, motioning for me to follow. I crowd in and she gives a little groan as we squish together, then we both go still, listening.

"Yeah," Zeke answers. "Just my nephew's girl. I sent her on home."

"All right." Now I hear the crackle of leaves and the swish of branches, and Zeke's reply is fainter. "Told her I'd tell her daddy on her if she came back."

Neither of them speaks again and their footsteps fade until all I can hear is the burbling of the creek and the breeze through the trees.

Once again, Molly cautiously climbs out and peeks around the tree. I have a nice, rousing shake and Molly looks at me in alarm, her finger to her lips. But no one is near. I could tell her that if only I could speak.

She quietly looks around and then finally relaxes a little. "Why'd he run us off from these woods?" she asks in a whisper. "What's he so worried about? And he said his cousin owned the land, but I kind of remember that all the land by the creek was state forest."

I can't answer any of her questions, of course, so I get another drink instead.

Molly takes out her camera and clicks it in the direction of the tree, the stream, the hill that Lizzie came down, and the place where the stream narrows—the direction that Zeke came and left from.

"I wonder why he was so upset." Click, goes her camera. Click. Click. "Like he was afraid of something."

Suddenly, she shoves the camera in her pocket, and grabs her phone, studying it for a second. "Oh my gosh. Dinner! We're late!" She takes off at a run. I trot alongside her, enjoying the chance to stretch my legs.

By the time we run up the last little rise to the house, Molly is red-faced and sweaty. I like the smell of her sweat, and am particularly fond of the way her socks smell after she wears them a few days. All in all, Molly has a very nice scent.

And another nice scent—actually a whole *noseful* of scents— are the ones coming from the house. We rush up to the porch, where the boss waits with an unhappy expression on his face. "Where have you been? We're all waiting on you."

"Sorry," Molly mumbles. "We got a little lost."

"How far did you *go?*" the boss asks

Molly mutters something as we hurry into the house, but frankly I'm not listening. I'm concentrating on the delicious smells coming from the kitchen. It's amazing what cooking does for turkey. Can't help but drool a little.

Pretty soon everyone—meaning all the people—are seated at the table. Bridger and I are on the floor as usual, awaiting our turn.

Marmie says, "Can we hold hands for the blessing?"

Everyone takes a hand, and then Marmie says a prayer. I know about prayers from my service dog days. Sometimes our trainers would take us to churches to get used to being there. We learned that even when people are shouting out things like "Amen" and "Hallelujah", they don't want dogs joining in with a few well-timed barks. Just sayin'.

But no one shouts tonight, although there are some sighs of anticipation after the blessing when the plates of food get passed around, and then exclamations of how great it all tastes.

"Lizzie's family doesn't celebrate Thanksgiving anymore," Molly says, between forkfuls. "Or Christmas."

"Really?" The boss shakes his head and sighs. "How do you know that?"

Molly's fork stops halfway to her mouth, and her voice has that tiny quiver that means she's nervous about what she's saying. "Um, she told me. When we were at her house."

If the boss were paying attention, he would see that she clearly isn't telling the truth. But his head is bent as he slathers butter on his roll. "Why not?"

"Zeke says they shouldn't celebrate man-made holidays."

"But Christmas!" Marmie shakes her head. "That must be hard on the kids."

Molly nods agreement.

The boss lifts his glass of diet ginger ale, and stares into it. "I just don't understand," he says. "Will, of all people. Not that he's found a new religion—people do that all the time. Just that he's so ... so closed to anything outside it."

"Lizzie says Zeke is mean. He yells at them."

The boss turns to her, frowning slightly. "You found out a lot for the short time we were there."

"Yeah." Molly turns to the turkey on her plate with sudden interest and begins to cut it into pieces.

I must have drifted off to sleep, because the next thing I know I hear the sound of chairs scraping as everyone gets up from the table. And soon, Bridger and I are enjoying our bowls of food. Kibble, of course, because we always get that, but Marmie has ladled a fair amount of drippings, turkey skin, bits of meat, as well as bits of potatoes and gravy and even a piece of roll.

I finish my food with gusto, and soon we're all taking a nap by the fire in the family room, us dogs on the floor and the people slouched on the furniture.

I can see why this holiday is called Thanksgiving. There's lots to be thankful for.

Chapter 5

The Dos Amigos

Today's the day," Molly says the next morning, after I've come back from my rounds with Bridger. Her eyes brim with excitement. "I get to see Uncle Armando."

Sounds good to me because, according to Molly, Armando runs this great Mexican restaurant, although Molly seems to be more interested in the fact that he's a relative than that he owns a restaurant.

"He's not my real uncle," she tells Tanya on the phone before we leave. "He's actually my mom's cousin, but he's older than she is, and ever since I was little, I've always called him uncle."

As soon as Molly found out we were coming to the mountains, she began pestering the boss to visit her other Mexican relatives who still live in Laurel Woods.

"They're part of my family, too," she always says. "And I haven't seen them since Mom … left." To which he usually responds that it would be incredibly awkward for him. "I dropped contact with them after that," he reminds her. "Just too … hard. And they never thought much of me."

But, as usual, when Molly *really* wants something, the boss eventually caves, and he finally agreed to a visit while we're in Laurel Woods.

Before we go, the boss packs for a deer hunting trip he's going to take with his brother Matt and Grandjum. He's as excited about this as Molly is about seeing her Uncle Armando. "It's going to be the three of us, just like old times," he says more than once.

Molly meanwhile spends time at her computer, studying her photos—a normal thing for her, although one I frankly find boring. "I wonder where that leads to," she says. "Where Zeke came from? He was so busy asking us why we were in the woods, but he never said how he happened to be strolling along by himself in the middle of nowhere."

Can't answer that, but fortunately Molly doesn't expect me to.

When it's time to go, Molly asks if I can go too. "I wanted Uncle Armando to meet him."

"I guess. It's cool enough he can stay in the van."

Have I mentioned that the boss is often a killjoy? But at least he said yes.

Molly loads me in my crate, and we're off. The van winds around some narrow mountain roads, but fortunately I don't get sick.

"Dad," Molly says. Whoa. Suddenly I can smell her tension. "Remember the woods along Sycamore Creek below Lizzie's? Do you know who owns that?"

"I'm pretty sure that's state forest," the boss says without hesitation. "Why?"

"Just wondering."

The boss gives her a curious look and Molly flushes.

"Well, Lizzie told me that Zeke says his cousin owns it and won't allow her to go there anymore. That it's private property."

"I bet it's really because of Adam's accident. Will has kept a pretty tight rein on the kids ever since. And I don't blame him. I'm sure he doesn't want to take a chance with Lizzie being near water. So maybe Zeke was just saying that as a reason to keep her from going there."

"Yeah," Molly says, clearly not agreeing with this. But the boss is oblivious as always, and soon the van slows down because we're coming into town.

Lots of great smells as we pass the fast food places, kind of spoiled by the fumes from the gas stations. After a bit, Molly jumps a little in her seat and points to a sign on the opposite side of the road. "There it is! Los Dos Amigos!"

Above the lettering of the sign is a picture of two men with long, curling moustaches, both wearing giant hats, both with wide grins. One of the them holds up a taco and the other a drink, in one of those glasses that look like a little bowl with a long stem. A host of smells hit my nose: food as delicious as our turkey dinner the night before, but different. Mexican. Can't remember if I mentioned it, but I learned to like Mexican food—as well as all kinds of take-out including Chinese and wings, bones and all—with my second boss—the bad one. He usually fell asleep before he finished his food and I got to polish off what was left.

Molly hops out of the van almost before the boss turns off the engine. She opens the van's sliding door and is snapping on my leash when a man rushes towards us. "*Hola, Amigos!*" he says in a deep voice. "So glad you could come!" He looks like a more compact, older version of one of the men in the sign.

His hair is mostly gray, as is his moustache, which is neatly trimmed and considerably shorter than the twirling ones in the sign.

"Maria!" the man exclaims.

"Uncle Armando!" she squeals. Everyone is so excited that I have to bark.

"Doodle, hush," the boss says sharply. Easier said than done with all this emotion flying about.

The man opens his arms and lifts Molly in a big twirling hug. Normally she doesn't like that sort of thing, but she giggles in delight. He sets her down. "When I last saw you, you were this high." He holds his hand about knee level. Whoa. What's this? His eyes fill with tears. I don't think he's sad—he certainly doesn't smell sad or anxious—and he looks at Molly like she's the best thing he's ever seen.

"Oh, how you've grown!" He studies her a second. "Do you go by Maria or Molly?"

"Molly," she says a bit apologetically.

It takes me a moment to remember that Maria is one of Molly's names. "Maria is for my mother's side of the family," she likes to say, "and Maureen comes from my dad's grand-mother." I didn't understand that for a long time until I heard her tell Tanya that Molly is a nickname for Maureen. Kind of like when people call me the The Dude for Doodle. Molly usually adds that she's a hybrid like me. "You're poodle and Labrador retriever and I'm Mexican and Irish."

Armando turns to the boss, who's rubbing his beard, his face tight with tension.

"Hello," he says stiffly to Armando, and offers his hand.

But Armando pulls the boss into a big hug. "So good to see you, Josh. It's been too long."

"Doodle, hush," the boss commands when Armando releases him. Oops. Molly picks up the leash and opens the door to the crate.

I hop out of the van and stretch.

"So this is the world famous labradoodle!" Armando squats down to scratch me under my chin in the way that I particularly like. He smells of onion, garlic, peppers, and some kind of men's cologne. He's wearing jeans and a black shirt under a brightly colored vest and has shiny black shoes. He talks with a slight Spanish accent.

The boss laughs. "Hardly world famous, or we'd be rich."

"A crime fighter, I hear," the man says, still stroking me. He turns to Molly. "I am so sorry, but Mariela is in Atlanta. Our daughter Gloria—I doubt either of you'd remember her—just had her fourth child. But she sends her love and told me I have to take pictures and get you to promise to come again when she's in town."

Molly nods, a flicker of disappointment passing over her face.

"So," the boss gestures at the restaurant, "I hear you own this now."

Armando nods. "My father passed away several years ago, and Hector, his partner—the other original *Amigo*—" he waves a hand at the sign—"was in his seventies and wanted to retire. So I bought him out of his share and now I own it." He gives a rueful smile. "Or at least the bank does. Shall we go in? I'll give you the grand tour. And we have a very special lunch prepared for you."

"Can we bring Doodle?" Molly asks.

"It's cool enough he can stay in the van." As I said, the boss is always quick to be a killjoy. But he's right about the temperature. Clouds have rolled in under a chilly breeze.

Armando glances down at me, a slight frown forming between his eyes.

"I could put his vest on, the one that says he's a working dog, so he'd be official," Molly says quickly, seeing his hesitation.

"Good idea. In case anyone wonders why I let a dog into the place. I don't like to think that the board of health is tougher on my place than Billy Bob's Barbecue down the road, but—" an expression of pain passes through his eyes—"in my experience it pays to be careful." The frown eases into a smile.

"But—" the smile fades—"does the vest say he's a bed bug dog? That'd be the last thing I need."

Molly says, "We have a plain one, that doesn't say Hunter Bed Bug Detection. We could use it and say he's a therapy dog. There are lots of those these days. Or a dog that predicts epileptic attacks."

The boss's eyebrows raise as he looks at his daughter in mild astonishment. "I hope you don't plan to go into a life of crime," he says under his breath. "Did we even bring that vest?"

Molly looks embarrassed. I'm not sure why. Crime? "I stuck it in his box," she says, "in case we needed it."

She rummages through a box in the van and comes back with my plain vest, and pretty soon we're all walking through the doors into the wonderful, meaty, cheesy, garlicky, peppery air of the restaurant.

"Welcome to Dos Amigos," Armando says, opening his arm and bowing just a little.

We walk into a room with a hard tile floor that smells faintly of disinfectant. Armando leads us past booths and shiny wood tables that regrettably don't have any bits of food underneath them, to a door in the back. Music fills the room, someone singing in Spanish. I know a little Spanish from both my service dog days and my time with my trainer, Miguel, but not enough to understand the singer. It's clear, though, from the anguish in his voice, that the man is suffering. I suppress a whine. Never have liked it when things get too emotional.

We follow him to a booth in the back. Armando and the boss sit on one side of the table, and Molly on the other, holding my leash. I had lots of restaurant training in my service dog days, so I know the drill. I lie down quietly next to Molly. Restaurants aren't places a dog is allowed to bark, or even stand up and sniff around. Unless we're looking for bed bugs, of course.

Armando waves his arm and soon a young woman brings drinks and bowls of chips and salsa to the table. Salsa is always a little tricky. It can be good, but sometimes it can really burn your mouth, so you need to smell it carefully before eating it. Chips are always tasty, of course. Not that I'm getting any of either at the moment. But Molly is good to slip me bites from time to time, so I stay alert.

With a flourish, under Armando's beaming gaze, the waitress sets a couple of soda cans and a tall glass of ice in front of the boss.

The boss's eyebrows lift in surprise. "Diet ginger ale!"

"I got some in especially for you. And Pepsi for Molly, as usual. And I have ordered all your favorites. Armando Federico Vega doesn't forget what his customers—and especially his *family*—like!"

For a moment, the boss looks uncomfortable—no, guilty— like a dog caught with his nose in the trash—but then he relaxes. "Thanks."

The waitress disappears and then returns, staggering slightly under the weight of a large round tray filled with food. People are starting to filter in and the sound of their conversation partially drowns out the music. A good thing because now a woman is singing, and by the sound of it, she's worse off than the man.

Armando dabs at his moustache with his napkin, and leans towards Molly. "So, I hear that you're a detective, too. That you found your mother."

"Word certainly gets out around here," the boss murmurs.

Armando laughs. "You don't understand the Mexican gossip network. Faster than Google. *La Habladera,* we call it."

This gets even the boss to crack a smile, although I'm not sure why.

"You know," Armando says, suddenly serious, "that your mother hasn't talked to her father—your *abuelo*—since the big fight."

"Big fight?" Molly straightens up, sets down a chip and begins to twist a bit of her hair, a sure sign that she's nervous. But then this is no surprise—discussing her mother always does this to her. I've never figured out why.

"You have not heard of the big fight?" Armando glances at the boss, who rubs his beard but says nothing. "Your mother, she wanted to stay here in the U.S. But your grandfather had different ideas. He wanted her to go back to Mexico with the family. He said since she was a natural born citizen, she could come back later, in a few years, but the family needed her now. And she was too young to marry." He shakes his head. "Your mother said if she left, she'd never afford to come back and she wasn't going back to Mexico to live like a peasant the rest of her life."

Molly nods, her fingers twisting away at her hair. "She told me she thought she'd never be able to get an education down there."

Armando sets his napkin on the table. "I'm afraid she might have been right—at least at that time. But your *abuelo* is, or at least was, a very macho man. *Machísimo, comprendes?*"

Molly nods again, her eyes intent on Armando.

"And hot tempered. He got very angry that his daughter would dare challenge him. He ordered her to go, told her she had no choice." Armando takes a sip of water, once again presses his napkin to his moustache and then tilts his head toward the boss. "And so your *padre*—your daddy, as they like to say here in the South—who is every bit as stubborn as your *abuelo*—stole away with your mother in the night, and when they returned, they were married. And your grandfather could do nothing about it. And your mother hasn't spoken to him since."

Molly stares at him, then turns to the boss. "You *eloped*? You never told me. Or about the fight."

Once again, the boss has that hang-dog look. "Sorry," he says at last. "Didn't seem important."

Molly's eyes widen in disbelief.

Armando leans forward, twirling his glass with his fingers. "It was important to *us*—to all the family," he says softly. "But I don't think back then you cared much for Cori's family."

"No, I didn't." The boss looks stricken. "Not because Cori's family was Mexican," he hastens to add. "That truly didn't matter. I grew up in Arizona and half my friends were Mexican. I just saw her parents as an obstacle to our getting married." He shakes his head ruefully. "I was young. We were all so young. For the record, my parents were as upset as Cori's when we ran off and got married."

Molly says, "How come no one ever told me? Marmie never said a word."

The boss shrugs. "It's not a favorite topic of conversation."

Armando says, "I know not everyone here in Laurel Woods was happy about you marrying a *Mejicano*, but I never felt you cared about that. And we don't mind that our precious Corazón married an Anglo—" he smiles at the boss—"as long as we get to see our Molly."

Molly's face flushes at this, but her eyes sparkle. They talk some more, but I don't see any chips coming my way, so I doze off.

And then, Molly suddenly goes rigid. *Lizzie,* she says under her breath. I lift my head. Sure enough, Lizzie, along with her entire family, and Zeke, the bad Zeke, are being shown to a table just up from our booth.

Chapter 6

Turning Up the Heat

ARMANDO RISES AND GIVES WILL A LITTLE WAVE. "Welcome *señores* and *señora*," he says with a broad smile. "One sweet tea?" he asks Nettie, who nods and smiles back. "Two orange sodas?" He dips his head at Lizzie and Becca. "And two unsweet teas, right?" Will and Zeke both nod.

The boss eases out from the booth and goes up to their table. "Hi, Will. Nettie. Good to see you. I'm ... sorry about yesterday. I didn't mean to ... overstep." I can hear the strain in his voice. Will stares at him, his face expressionless.

Zeke looks straight at the boss, then, without a word, sits down and lifts his menu in front of his face. Will gives the boss a curt nod, and mimics Zeke. Nettie flashes the boss an apologetic smile, then turns her attention to seating her children.

The boss, flushing deeply, turns and scoots back into the booth.

Armando murmurs something under his breath, excuses himself, and disappears into the kitchen. Molly and the boss stare at their plates in silence.

When Armando returns, he asks in one of those fake-cheerful voices that humans sometimes use, "So, tell me, Josh, how are your folks doing? I think they've given up eating Mexican food."

"Good," the boss says in a distracted voice. "Well, you know. They were embarrassed to come back here after..."

Molly picks up her fork and takes a bite, and everyone seems to relax a little. I lay my head back down, ready to take another nap, but just as I'm dozing off, I hear the scrape of a chair against the tile. Lizzie gets up and goes across the restaurant to a hallway on the opposite side. Molly watches her go, and then suddenly rises. "Excuse me. I need to use the restroom."

"You know where it is." Armando tilts his head toward the direction that Lizzie just went, a smile tugging at the corners of his mouth.

Molly crosses the room and disappears through the same doorway.

"Where is *she* going?" Zeke demands, a sour expression on his face. He's watching the doorway.

Will frowns, his head bent over his plate.

Zeke keeps glancing at the door. Finally, he says in a peeved voice, "Nettie, I think you ought to go check on Lizzie."

"I'm sure she'll be back soon," Nettie says, biting her lip a little.

Will looks up at her. "Would you please go check on our daughter?"

With a tiny sigh, Nettie stands and heads towards the restroom, but just then Lizzie comes out, grinning broadly.

Both her dad and Zeke glare at her as she sits down at the table, but neither says anything. And then Molly returns, also looking quite cheerful.

The boss gives her a speculative glance.

Molly asks in a bright voice, "So, your father—my grandfather's uncle, right?—and this Hector started Dos Amigos?"

"That's right. Not here. Back then, the only Latinos here were migrant workers and there weren't too many of them. They started the restaurant in Tucson, Arizona—" the boss looks up in surprise and Armando nods—"that's right."

"He was legal?" Molly asks. "Your father?"

Armando spreads his hands. "Well, when he came over—it was in the fifties, remember—he wasn't. But he learned English, worked hard, and got amnesty in the late eighties. Plus, he married my mother, who was born in Tucson and already a citizen."

"So when did you come up here to the mountains," the boss asks.

"Not until—when was it?" Armando scratches his chin—"2000, I think. But your grandfather came to Tucson before that—in the eighties, I think—to work for him."

"1985," Molly says with certainty. "The year my mother was born. Another few months and she wouldn't have been a citizen."

"Ah. I didn't remember exactly. I was a young man—" He stops, his attention drawn by a choking, sputtering sound.

Zeke, fork in air, coughs and spews his food onto his plate, his face dark. He grabs his tea, takes a few big gulps, and then turns to Armando. "Holy s—" He lets out a string of words the boss calls "language," and several people in nearby tables raise their heads and stare. "What'd you *do* to this?" he sputters between coughs. "It's too hot to eat!"

Armando jumps to his feet. "I'm so sorry. *Lo siento. Lo siento.* We have a new cook. My deepest apologies. I will not charge you—" he waves a hand at the whole group—"*any* of you for this meal." He picks up the plate and signals to a waiter who rushes over to take it. He hands him the plate, turning so his back is to Zeke and everyone at the table. "Tell Alberto this is unacceptable," he says in a loud voice, but he has a faint smile on his face as he says it. The waiter hurries off, plate in hand.

Armando follows the waiter, returning before long with a new plate of food for Zeke. Chicken fajitas by the smell of it. He sets it down before the man, apologizing again, then comes back to our table and sits down, his black eyes alive with anticipation. I watch him carefully because clearly, by his body language, something is going to happen. And it does, although not from Armando.

"What the f—?" Zeke shoots up from his chair, glowering at Armando as he lets out another stream of "language." "Are you trying to *kill* me? There's enough salt in this chicken to be a deer lick."

Armando shakes his head, holding out his hands as if totally baffled. "I don't understand. I told Alberto to take extra care, to make your dish *perfecto*." Armando's Spanish accent has suddenly thickened. "It ees hard to find good help these days. But *lo siento*. As I said, no charge for anyone here, *comprende*? Everything is free, *gratis*."

Zeke throws his napkin over his plate and drains the last few swallows from his tea. "Damn right there's no charge because we're not going to eat this crap. And you can be sure we'll never come here again." He gestures to Will. "Come on. We're done." Becca emits a squeal of protest that fades under Zeke's withering glare.

Zeke turns and stalks toward the door, Will on his heels. Except for yet another distressed singer wailing in the background, the restaurant is now dead silent, everyone's attention locked on Will's family.

Lizzie stuffs some chips into her pocket and a big bite of taco into her mouth as she slowly gets to her feet, and Becca follows her example, grabbing what food she can before hurrying after her father and Zeke, who have already made it to the door. Nettie gives Armando an apologetic smile and then joins her family. Just before she disappears through the door, Lizzie nods towards Molly and gives her a thumbs up sign, which Molly quickly returns. I had a trainer who used to do that whenever we got something right, but I have no idea what's going on here.

"Well," the boss says, after they've all left and the chatter in the restaurant starts to return to normal. "That was ... interesting. Do you think Zeke was making that up?"

Armando shakes his head, shrugging. "Who knows? I'll have a talk with the cook later." He relaxes against the back of the booth, takes a bite of his enchilada, and launches into a series of stories about Molly's family in Mexico.

Molly leans forward and listens intently, ignoring the food on her plate. I doze off, waking up every so often to see if Molly wants to give me any of her meal, but no luck.

Lunch lasts a long time. Finally, the boss checks his watch. "Think I'll use the facilities, and then we really need to get back. Matt should be arriving before too long."

Armando jumps up to let the boss out and I sit up just to remind Molly I'm here and willing to help her clean her plate.

When he's gone, Molly says, "That was really nice of you to pay for all of Will's family's lunch. I mean, the only one with bad food was Zeke, and he might have just been making it up."

Armando grins, an amused expression in his eyes. "Well, if you wreck someone's meal, you can't expect them to pay for it."

Molly nods and opens her mouth to speak, but Armando interrupts. "Especially if you do it on purpose."

Now Molly's mouth stays open in surprise. "On purpose?" she asks at last.

He winks at her, a gesture that frankly I've never quite understood. "Anyone who insults my family, like Zeke did to your father, is not welcome in my restaurant."

"But they'll probably never ever come back."

Armando shrugs. "So much the better. But this is our secret, no? The county health department might not agree with my methods."

"Cross my heart," Molly says, nodding.

Another baffling remark.

Before long the boss returns and everyone hugs and promises to keep in touch, and then we're back in the van heading back to Marmie's and Grandjum's.

Chapter 7

Reunion

WHEN WE GET BACK, MOLLY HELPS MARMIE PACK a dinner for the men, while the boss and Grandjum start loading Grandjum's pickup with stuff for a deer-hunting trip.

"Matt should be here by four," the boss says, consulting his watch, something he keeps doing every few minutes. I've heard the boss talk about his brother Matt, of course, but haven't met him. According to the boss, he and his family couldn't come for Thanksgiving dinner because it was their turn to spend it with his wife's family, but he took a few extra days off for the hunting trip.

"It's going to be great," the boss keeps saying, almost as often as he checks his watch.

I think if they want to find deer their best bet would be to take me along. I'm the one with the nose after all. But the boss repeats his tiresome phrase about me and guns not being a good mix, so I'm to stay home with Molly and Marmie. Bridger has to stay as well because they think he's too old and will get tired. So, they're going to go tramp around the woods looking for creatures that would be easy to find if they had a decent sense of smell. They might as well go blindfolded. And don't blame us dogs if they come back empty-handed. Just sayin'.

While they pack and Marmie loads an ice chest, Molly goes to her room and shuts the door, forgetting me, which is unusual. I scratch lightly on the door.

"Oh, Doodle. Sorry!" She lets me in, swishing the door shut behind me. Her phone is up to her ear and I hear Stu's voice coming through, saying something about napping.

"Oh. Well, don't wake her up. But will you guys be home tomorrow around one-thirty or two? If we wanted to visit?"

"Sure. Louisa doesn't usually lie down until around three. But call first, will you? In case she's having a bad day. I know she'd love to see you, but some days she's just not up to company."

"Okay, I'll call first," Molly says, snapping her phone shut. Then she freezes for a second, hand in mid-air and opens it again and presses a key. She listens until a voice comes on the line—hey, it's Cori—at least it's her voice. But all it says is "Please leave a message."

Molly hesitates, then says, "Hey. It's me, Molly, again. I ... I hope you had a good Thanksgiving. I tried to call, but didn't get you. I saw Uncle Armando yesterday, and wanted to tell you about the visit." A pause. "Okay, bye." And she snaps the phone shut with a sigh. I go over to her and give her fingers a lick.

I've mentioned before that I'm not really a touchy-feely type dog, but when her whole body goes slack with disappointment, I can't help but remind her I'm here and if we did something fun like go for a walk, she'd probably feel better.

She doesn't take the hint—at least not at first, because the boss shouts, "Matt's here!" and we all go outside as an SUV pulls up to the house. A man steps out who looks like a taller, heavier version of the boss and Grandjum.

"Matt!" the boss rushes over to give him a hug, and then Matt hugs Marmie and Grandjum, and Molly.

"And this is Doodle, Uncle Matt," Molly says.

"The infamous labradoodle!" Matt exclaims. "Keep your weapons away from him!"

Seriously, I don't know where all this stuff comes from. It was not my fault either time that I got shot.

We all go inside, but not for long. The boss calls Annie to tell her that he's leaving and probably won't have cell phone reception for a few days. And then he and Matt and Grandjum climb into Grandjum's truck, and Molly and Marmie wave as they drive away.

Not long after, Molly asks if she can take a walk. "I'd like to get some pictures of the trees," she says.

Marmie, who's sitting in her favorite chair, holding a cup of tea that emits faint tendrils of steam, says, "I guess that'd be okay. Will you be going in the woods?"

"A little." Molly's hand strays up to twist a strand of hair.

"Hold on." She bustles out of the room and comes back carrying a bright vest and scarf. "Deer hunting season started last week. Better wear this if you're in the woods. We don't have many hunters round here, but it doesn't hurt to be safe." She hands Molly the vest, which hangs down past her hips. Then she ties the scarf around my neck. "I wouldn't want him to be mistaken for a bear!"

So, we get our walk after all, me wearing my "don't-shoot-me" scarf and Molly with her bright vest. And, hey, turns out we're going back to where she and Lizzie met the other day.

When we get there, Molly hurries over to the tree with the hollow, bending down and raking her fingers through the leaves inside.

"Yes!!" she exclaims. She pulls out an envelope and quickly opens it, then reads aloud:

> "Dear Molly, OK we're on for tomorrow. Daddy's gonna be gone for most of the day putting in a furnace for some rich doctor and Mama always takes a nap 'bout that time. And I checked out Adam's old bike and it works fine. See you at Squirrel Nut road at one. If I don't show up, something happened. Love, Lizzie."

Molly pulls a pen from the inside pocket of her jacket and, balancing the note on her knee, writes something, and then sticks the note back in the envelope and back under the leaves in the hollow.

I'm not sure what's going on, but Molly seems much happier. I knew a walk would do the trick.

The next day, Molly is as nervous as a cat meeting a German shepherd. She helps Marmie clean out the fridge while Bridger and I watch, hoping for some tidbits. We end up with bites of stuffing, turkey skin, and some vegetable dish that's not as good as the meat, but still worth eating.

Just before lunch, Molly slips to her room and makes a call. "Hey, it's Molly," she says, when Stu's voice comes on the line. She holds the phone in one hand while twisting a strand of hair in the other and I can hear her heart speed up. "Is it okay if we come today?"

"We'd love to see you!" Stu says. "Louisa's having a good day. And tell your dad we have some of Turner's Key lime pie for him when he comes."

The boss is going with us? I thought Marmie said the men wouldn't be back until evening.

"Um, okay." Molly swallows. "We'll see you around 1:30 or 2:00."

During lunch, Molly does a lot of hair twisting and very little eating, so I end up with most of her turkey sandwich. Bridger misses out, as he's lying on the floor on the other side of the table—too far away for Molly to slip him anything.

As soon as the last dish is put in the dishwasher, Molly says, "I think Doodle and I will take a little walk. While you take your nap."

Marmie smiles. "You know me well! Be sure and wear your vest."

So, Molly suits us up, but doesn't go outside right away. When Marmie goes to her room, she hurries outside, me beside her. "You stay home, Bridger," she says, shutting the door in his face. Poor dog misses out again.

Instead of taking off as we usually do, Molly circles around to the backside of the garage, an old bike is leaning against the wall. How'd that get there?

She hops on the bike and takes off, quickly at first as she sails down the hill, then very slowly going up the next one. We go along this way—fast downhill and slow up—until we come to the paved road.

We must not be going to Lizzie's because Molly turns in the opposite direction. She stops to put me on leash and then gets on her bike again. "Heel!" she commands. "I don't want you to pull me over." We go slow, mostly because we're climbing a hill. As soon as we get to the top, I'm looking forward to speeding up again, but Molly only goes a little faster. "Don't pull!" she shouts, yanking the leash a little. "Heel!" Oh. I drop back to a heeling position and she holds out a treat. That's what I like about heeling, even though I prefer to be in front, to lead the pack so to speak.

Molly stops at a crossroad that's about halfway down the hill. On one side it's paved and on the other, it's a wide gravel road. Suddenly, I recognize it. Lizzie's driveway!

She pulls off the road and dismounts, pushing down the kickstand so the bike doesn't fall over, then checks her phone. "No message," Molly says. She frowns, staring down the paved side of the road, then moves the bike further off the road. She checks her phone again. And again.

In the distance, down the gravel road, I hear the sound of a car. Something about it sounds familiar. Where have I heard it? As it gets closer, I remember. Zeke's truck.

Now, Molly hears it, too. "Quick!" She grabs the bike and runs across the main road, turning the bike toward Marmie's. Zeke's truck roars over the hill and squeals to a stop at the crossroad amid a cloud of exhaust. Rocky, in the back, starts barking furiously. The hair rises on my back.

"Leave it," Molly says in a low voice. She glances quickly at the truck and then pedals hard up the hill, not looking back. Are we going home already?

The truck turns onto the road and soon is beside us, sending Rocky into new rounds of hysteria. Zeke rolls down his window. "Rocky, shut up!" And then, in a shout to be heard over Rocky, who doesn't quiet down at all, "What're y'all doing out here?"

"Just taking Doodle out for some exercise," Molly says, her voice so strained that the hair on my back rises even higher. Come to think about it, I can feel her tension through the leash. I wonder if she's afraid of Rocky. "Heading back now."

Zeke stares at her, his watery eyes filled with speculation. "Does your daddy know you're here? This ain't a safe road for bikes. No shoulder."

"It's just for a tiny bit, and then we get on a side road," Molly says.

He grimaces and then guns the engine. "Good thing you ain't my kid," he shouts as the truck roars off.

Molly stands by the side of the road until the sound of the truck is long gone. Not the smells, of course. Gas fumes, oil, dust, sweat, not to mention Rocky's pungent odor still hang in the air.

Finally, Molly turns the bike and we go back to the crossroads. She checks her phone, sighs, checks her phone again.

And then I hear something else on the road. Not a car, but the bumpy squishy sound of tires on pavement.

"What is it, Doodle?" Molly asks, staring down the road.

A figure comes over the hill. I relax when I see it's Lizzie.

"You made it!" Molly says with considerable relief when Lizzie has pulled up beside us, red-faced and breathing hard.

"Almost didn't," she answers. "Zeke drove up just as I was leaving, wantin' to know where Daddy was. So I just circled around the driveway a few times and then put the bike back in the shed and came in like I was done riding. And he had to talk to Mama forever, tryin' to get a check from her because his power bill was due. But she told him that Daddy had the checkbook and he'd have to get it from him and then she had to tell him how to get to Dr. Weisscroft's, and I sat there and about died. And finally he left, but Mama asked me to empty the trash. I thought for sure you'd be gone by now."

"He saw me," Molly says, grimacing. "But when I heard the

truck, I turned around and told him I was on my way home." She checks her phone. "Almost one-thirty. We better get going."

They both get on their bikes, and this time we cross the road and go straight onto the dirt road, which is plenty bumpy for the bikes but easier on my paws than the pavement. It's a glorious day for a ride. The sun's bright in a clear sky, and the bare trees cast dark shadows that line the road like uneven ribs. The scent of leaves fills my nose. And while the air has a chill, there's no wind. I'm able to work up a bit of a pant.

After a bit, we turn onto a long driveway that seems familiar. After another hill I realize why. We've come to Stu and Louisa's house.

The girls pull up to the front steps and get off their bikes, just as Stu is opening the door.

For a moment, he stares, his face wide with surprise. Then he says, "I don't believe it." Then, "*Lizzie!*" He runs to Lizzie and picks her up in a fierce embrace. "Oh, Lizzie!" He carries her through the open door, saying in a loud voice, "Guess who I got here?"

Louisa gives a squeal of delight. Molly and I follow them inside. The place still reeks of cats, but I see no sign of them. Lizzie leans over Louisa's wheelchair, her arms around her grandmother.

"Hey, Mamaw," Lizzie says. "I've missed you."

"Oh, my darling, you don't know how much I've missed you. This is truly an answer to a prayer." Louisa's eyes fill with tears. "I'm so glad your daddy finally allowed you to come. Josh said he'd talk to him, but I didn't believe it'd do any good."

Molly and Lizzie exchange a worried look.

"Well," Lizzie says at last, "Daddy doesn't exactly know I'm here. Molly and me kind of decided to come on our own."

More silence and more worried glances, this time between Louisa and Stu. "Oh, honey." Stu shakes his head. "I'm not sure that was the right thing to do."

"I am." Louisa gives her husband a defiant look. "I am so *very* glad I got to see at least one of my grandbabies before … well, you know."

"That's what we thought," Molly says.

Lizzie nods agreement. "And Daddy don't need to know about us being here."

"Well, he won't know from us," Stu says. "Not that I really approve of you going behind his back, no matter what I think about him. But you know Zeke's trailer is just one ridge over."

Molly casts an anxious glance at the window.

"He said he was going to where Daddy's working," Lizzie says.

"To work?" Louisa gives a bitter laugh. "That'll be the day."

"No, to get a check from him."

"That I believe." Louisa adjusts the blanket on her lap and I notice her hands are shaking. "But, how'd y'all get here? I thought Josh and Molly were coming over."

"Bikes," Molly says, still staring at the window. "My dad's deer hunting. With Uncle Matt and Grandjum."

Stu frowns in surprise, his cheeks puffing out even more than usual. "Bikes! That's dangerous. There's no shoulder."

"We took Squirrel Nut—the dirt road. Didn't see a single car."

"I suppose." Louisa sounds unconvinced. "Maybe Stu could load your bikes in the truck and drive you home."

Both Lizzie and Molly seem alarmed by this. "No!" they say simultaneously. Molly adds, "We'll be okay. Hardly anyone ever uses that road. But I think—" another glance at the window— "maybe we shouldn't stay too long. In case Zeke gets back."

"At least have a little of the Key lime pie I promised your daddy," he says, looking at Molly. "Store bought but good anyway."

"None for me, dear," Louisa says, adjusting the blanket over her knees. Stu goes off to the kitchen while Louisa talks softly to Lizzie and I doze. Before long, he comes back with a tray and three plates containing wedges of pie the color of new grass. Doesn't smell good to me at all, but Lizzie and Molly finish it off with gusto. Stu leaves some of his.

"Are you sure you don't want me to drive you?" he asks as he clears away the plates. "Just to your roads, and you can bike the rest of the way." He smiles conspiratorially. "So you don't have to explain where you've been."

"It's only two miles," Molly says, "which is nothing on a bike, and back roads almost the whole way except for a tiny stretch on Big Laurel Creek."

Stu sighs and looks up at his wife who says, "I used to bike all over the county when I was a kid. They'll be okay."

After another round of hugging and a few more tears from Louisa—but happy ones from the way she keeps smiling every time she looks at Lizzie—we go outside. And soon we're back on the road, the smell of leaves and dust and smoke in the air.

The girls ride in silence along the bumpy dirt road, slowing to a stop when they get to the pavement. Lizzie says, "Mamaw looked awful." She walks her bike onto the asphalt.

"Yeah," Molly agrees, doing the same. She calls me over and attaches the leash, and then they mount the bikes again, neither of them speaking until they come to Lizzie's driveway.

"Well," Lizzie says in a dejected voice, "have fun in Arlington."

"I'm sorry about your grandma," Molly says. She steps on the kickstand and comes over to Lizzie and they hug briefly.

Tears well in Lizzie's eyes. "I'm really glad I saw her. I *hate* Zeke."

In the distance, I hear the whine of an engine. Not Zeke's truck, which I'd recognize anywhere. I lift my head and listen.

Molly goes back to her bike just as a white pickup comes over the hill.

"Oh, no!" Lizzie's eyes go wide with consternation. "*Daddy*. What's he doing here *now*?"

Molly grabs her bike and jumps on. I'm right beside her, well, maybe a little ahead because before we've even made it to the road, I feel the tug of the leash as she stops. "Too late," she says, and the truck slows down and turns onto the road.

Will rolls down the window and stares at them, his jaw tight. "What's going on?" His eyes focus on Lizzie and then Molly in turn.

Neither says a word. Finally, Lizzie says in a small but defiant tone, "We was just going for a ride."

Will glowers at them both, then turns to Molly. "Does your Daddy know you're here? I can't believe he'd go behind my back like this. I made it clear that y'all weren't welcome—"

"No," Molly interrupts. "He's deer hunting. He doesn't know. He wouldn't— it's … my fault. My idea."

"Well, he'll know now. He'll know I don't appreciate him not keeping his kid in line." He pulls out his phone, then frowns, staring at it. "Deer hunting? Who's watching you?"

"Marmie," Molly says under her breath.

"Well, she'll know about it, too." He turns to Lizzie. "You're in a world of trouble, you know that."

Lizzie nods.

"Now get back to the house."

"Yes, sir," she says, her face flushed and angry. She climbs onto her bike and pedals toward her house.

"As for you," Will says to Molly, "I don't know if you got any rules in your family or if your daddy just lets you run wild. But I hope you know that you went and got Lizzie into a lot of trouble."

Molly meets his eyes, her face as flushed as Lizzie's. Whoa, and she's angry, too. I can smell it. The hair rises on my back. "My dad has lots of rules," she says in a voice so tight that I bump her palm with my nose to remind her I'm right here by her side. "Just not stupid ones like not being able to see my friends. Or my family, even when they're *dying*."

Will's mouth sags in disbelief. He shakes his head, and without another word, throws the truck into gear and takes off in a cloud of dust.

Molly stands straight as a tree until he's out of sight. Then she bends down and throws her arms around my neck. "Oh, Doodle." She buries her face in my fur. Oh no. She's crying. Her body shudders softly and after a bit I feel the moisture from her tears dampening my fur. When at last she pulls away, I give her face a few licks to clean it up, and then we're off again.

"He's wrong." she says, when we turn down Grandjum's long driveway. "I'm going to be in so much trouble."

Chapter 8

Big Trouble

IF BY BIG TROUBLE MOLLY MEANT EVERYONE WAS going to be mad at her, she was right.

When we pull up in front of the house, Marmie is standing on the porch, with a phone to her ear and a frown on her face. "Yes," she is saying. "Yes, I understand. I'll talk with her." The angry voice on the other end is Will's. "You can try his cell," Marmie says when there's a break in the torrent of words. "I don't know if he'll have reception or not, but you can try. And I'll certainly talk to him when he comes home tomorrow night."

Molly tries to slink past her through the door, but Marmie reaches out and grabs her arm, shaking her head at her. When Will finally gets off the phone, Marmie turns and begins to lecture Molly about sneaking off, lying, getting Lizzie in trouble, ruining her dad's hunting trip, and probably a few more things. I decide it's all a bit stressful for my taste, so I slip away and join Bridger for a nice nap in the late afternoon sun, over behind the house, mostly out of earshot.

Things remain tense between Molly and Marmie through dinner that night, especially when the boss returns Marmie's call and she tells him all about what happened.

After dinner, Molly stays in her room and works on a letter to Lizzie. "I just want to let her know how sorry I am she got in trouble, but I bet if I mail it, she'll never see it." She sighs. "But I gotta try."

I doze off, and the next thing I know, Molly's on her computer. Like I said about humans and their machines...

"Here's a Google map of the creek," she says when I touch my nose to her hand. "The whole area—hundreds of acres all the way to the road—is state forest except for one little plot." She points to the screen, but frankly I can't make out much and of course there's no scent. "Maybe that's his cousin's land like Zeke told us, but his cousin doesn't have the right to order people off state forest land. Know what I mean?"

Actually, I don't, but I tilt my head and listen.

"Tanya says maybe he was hunting and had a camp in the woods, but he wasn't wearing a vest or carrying a rifle."

She starts to type again and I doze off, waking when Molly turns off the light and crawls into bed.

I'm almost asleep when a sound makes me sit up. It's Molly, crying softly into her pillow. I push my nose against her face. "Oh, Doodle," she whispers, "go to bed." And so I do, but I listen until Molly's breath calms into the slow and steady rhythm of sleep. I don't like it when Molly's sad.

So, I'm relieved the next morning when, right after breakfast, Marmie folds Molly into her arms, and kisses the top of her head. "You know I love you, right?"

Molly, her face pressed against Marmie's chest, murmurs something I don't quite hear. Then she pulls away. "I'm sorry," she says.

Marmie gives her another hug and says, "I know. Lizzie's lucky to have you for a friend. Now go get ready for church. I think the men will be back around two."

In spite of the hugs, I notice Molly doesn't eat much lunch after church—which works out for me, as I get most of her turkey sandwich. She's jumpy as a toad, watching the driveway and twisting her hair.

And then Marmie calls, "They're back."

We go out to the porch and see the truck rumble up and squeak to a stop. The men step out of the truck in a flurry of door slamming and laughter. They all reek of smoke, insect repellent, gun oil, and I detect a faint scent of hot dogs and baked beans. The only scent missing is that of a buck or doe. No surprise there.

The boss doesn't say a word to Molly at first. Instead, he busies himself helping Matt and Grandjum unload the truck. Doesn't *speak* a word, although his body language says plenty. Humans, in my experience, are generally oblivious to body language, but maybe this time Molly isn't, because she stands hanging her head like a dog caught going through the trash.

Matt and Grandjum assure Marmie that they all had a wonderful time, and they crack a few jokes about their hunting abilities—how the SPCA would approve of the trip because no animal was harmed. The boss laughs with them, but his voice has a nervous edge that makes me uncomfortable.

Finally, when everything's put away and the truck's back in the garage, the men all tramp up the steps onto the porch, through the house and into the kitchen where Marmie has a pot of coffee brewing and is slicing pieces of pumpkin pie. Much better than Key lime, in my opinion.

"Molly," the boss says in a low voice. He tilts his head toward the family room and she follows him there. I'm torn. I don't like human conflict—makes me nervous and sometimes I just have to bark—plus there's always the possibility of getting a bite of pie if I stay in the kitchen—but Molly seems so worried that I reluctantly get up and pad after her. I get through the door just as the boss is closing it.

I think Molly and I are both waiting for the boss to yell, but instead he sighs and then puts his face in his hands. His body sags with exhaustion. It must have been a tiring trip. Finally, he says, still in a flat voice, "Do you want to explain?"

Molly bites her lip and twists an end of hair, but then haltingly tells the story—how Lizzie really wanted to see her grandmother, and how they'd planned the bike trip while Will was supposed to be gone, how first Zeke and then Will showed up at the wrong time.

While she talks, the boss never moves, but holds his head in his hands, staring at the floor. When she reaches the end, he turns toward her, rubbing his beard.

"You planned all this while you were in the restroom at Dos Amigos?"

Molly hesitates and then says in a strained voice, "Well, there and when we were at her house."

What? I guess she's forgotten about meeting Lizzie by the tree and all the notes she put in the hollow.

I can smell the salty, smoky sweat on the boss's skin, as he runs a dirt-streaked hand through his hair. "Will's furious at me. And you."

Molly doesn't answer.

"For all I think he's crazy right now listening to Zeke—I know this. Will *loves* his family. He wouldn't hurt them for the world."

"But he *is* hurting them." Molly's eyes brim with defiance.

"Maybe he is, maybe he isn't. But I know the last thing on earth he wants to do is hurt them." He rubs his eyes and then his beard. "It's tough to be a parent. Like driving in the fog, sometimes."

"I know." Molly takes a shaky breath. "But you should have seen how happy Louisa was. And Lizzie really, really wanted to see her ... before ... you know."

"I know." The boss's mouth forms a tight line. Another long silence. I feel a sudden need to scratch an ear, which I do.

"I don't know where to begin," he says at last. "Leaving aside all the stuff with Will and Lizzie, there's still such a list. You rode with the bike on the road with Doodle on the leash? He could have pulled you over."

"He was really good," Molly says. "He's had all that bike training with you, and he didn't pull once."

"And on Squirrel Nut—over all those bumps? You had him on leash then?"

It takes Molly a long time to answer. "No," she says finally, not looking at him.

The boss absorbs this without moving. "You let our $10,000 dog—which, by the way, I'm still paying off on the credit card—run loose in the woods?" He shakes his head. "I don't know how many times or ways I can tell you that Doodle is not a pet. He's the heart of our business and if something happens to him, we're broke. And I'll be in a dead-end job and you'll have to quit Tri-State Science Academy and go to public school." He pauses, then adds, "I said he could go free right around the house, but you know better than to have him off leash on a trip. What if he'd chased a squirrel and got lost?"

Get lost? I don't think so. After all, I have my superior nose. Molly, pale now, whispers, "I'm sorry."

"Sorry won't save us if something happens to Doodle."

"He never tried to run away."

The boss ignores this. "And then there's the fact that you were on Big Laurel Creek Road on a bike. There's no shoulder at all. If a truck came barreling around the corner—" He shuts his eyes and takes a deep breath.

"It was only for a tiny bit. Less than a quarter of a mile. All the other roads were dirt. We didn't see any cars. Well, except for Mr. Combs' truck."

"And then there's the fact that you basically lied to Marmie," the boss continues as if he hadn't heard. "I thought I raised you better than that."

At this, Molly takes a couple of ragged breaths and then swipes at her eyes with the sleeve of her blouse.

"I don't know what I'm going to say to Will," the boss continues, his eyes fixed on the far wall. "Maybe nothing. Maybe I don't have anything to say to him at all."

Whoa. Now he sounds angry.

"Who wouldn't allow his wife to see her dying mother? Or, for that matter, keep his kids from seeing their grandparents, sick or well? It's absurd. It's like we've dropped into the middle ages or something."

"Louisa was so happy to see Lizzie," Molly says, relief flooding her voice. "Even just for a little bit."

The boss turns to her and seems to notice her again. "Yeah," he says. "I don't think you were smart to do things the way you did, but of all the stuff you did today, that's the one thing I understand. Poor Lizzie. Poor Nettie. I'm surprised she doesn't tell Will off and just do it anyway." He clenches his fingers into a fist, then spreads them wide, straightening up and looking her in the eye.

"But that's not the point. Because of lying to Marmie, not keeping Doodle on the leash, and pretty much everything else, you're on restriction for the next month.

Molly stares at him. "*Month?* That"ll be through Christmas."

"That's right."

"But what about the Franklins' party?"

The Franklins are having a big Christmas party and Molly and Tanya have been rehearsing parts for a play they're going to put on. And I'm going to be in it because, according to Molly, my hair will be long enough that I'll look like a sheep. Why anyone would rather see a sheep than a dog is beyond me, but it seems to be a Christmas thing.

"But I invited Mom." She takes a deep breath. "I invited Mom and she said she'd come." Molly's eyes fill with new tears. "For the first time *ever.*"

"Too bad. Actions have consequences. Something you and Doodle *both* seem to have trouble learning."

Huh? Not sure what he means there.

"Anyway, even if Cori plans to come she'll probably get called to work and not be able to make it."

Molly looks so stricken that the boss sighs, scrunching up his face. "Sorry. I didn't mean that the way it sounded. I just hate for you to get your hopes up when you know she cancels more often than not. But—" He straightens and looks her in the eye, "that's to worry about in the future. For now, you're on restriction for a month."

"But Dad—" Her voice trails off because the boss has already risen and is walking toward the kitchen.

I get up and pad after him, remembering the pie and thinking Molly will be following, but she wheels around and marches to her room, slamming the door behind her. And this time, even when I scratch lightly and whine, she doesn't open it.

I try again a little later, after Bridger and I have had a few bits of piecrust and Matt's packing up his SUV to head for home. She cracks it open and lets me in. She's holding her phone to her ear. Her eyes are red and puffy, but when she speaks, her voice sounds almost normal.

Hey, it's Tanya at the other end.

"But you *have* to come to our party," Tanya says. "Maybe he'll change his mind."

"Maybe." Molly's voice doesn't hold much hope. "I wish I could talk to Lizzie. She's probably in worse trouble now and it's all my fault."

"Un-uh. You didn't make her do it. She decided to go same as you so it's not all your fault."

"It was my idea," Molly says, her face downcast.

"But she's got a brain, right? And she decided to do it. Mama always tells us it don't matter who has the idea, if we choose trouble it's our own fault for being stupid." She pauses a second. "Not that I'm calling you stupid. 'Cause I think you did the right thing to go. If someone tried to keep me from my dyin' grandma..."

Something in the way her voice comes over the line makes me almost see her for a second, her black eyes defiant and earnest.

Molly must hear it, too, because a tiny smile turns at the corner of her mouth, and she breathes a sigh of relief.

I circle down onto the wood floor by Molly's bed, wishing there was a nice soft rug like the one in Molly's room at home.

"It's all Zeke's fault," Molly says. "I mean not that I took Doodle on the bike and everything, but that we had to sneak out so Lizzie could see her grandmother. And Zeke's weird." She tells Tanya about Zeke finding them in the woods. "He ran us off like he owned the place and that's state forest land. We used to go there all the time. And what was he doing in the woods by himself? He didn't look like he was deer hunting. Why was he there?"

Tanya says, "Yeah, that's weird." Neither says anything for a bit. Then Tanya says, "I'll talk to Mama. Maybe she can work on your daddy—tell him all the great food she's going to cook for the party and how she needs our help 'cause she's workin' and everything. And how she was countin' on Doodle being there because he's her substitute dog." I raise my head at this. Love Mrs. Franklin. She's always good to me.

They talk some more. Molly tells Tanya about Lizzie's family and how everything's messed up there. "Dad thinks it's because of Adam. He says Mr. Combs fell apart after Adam drowned and that's how Zeke got hold of him."

"That could make him crazy all right," Tanya agrees.

Just then, the boss raps on the door. "Matt's ready to go."

So Molly says goodbye and I follow her out to see him off.

Chapter 9

Zeke

MARMIE HANDS MATT SEVERAL CONTAINERS OF food for his ice chest, and then everyone hugs and says goodbye. Matt even pats me on the head and strokes my back with his big hands. "You be a good boy, Doodle. Stay out of trouble."

As if I'd do anything else.

After Matt's gone, the boss pulls the van up right in front of the porch and starts packing his hunting gear. We're not going home until in the morning—the boss worries about getting caught in Sunday night traffic—but he wants to get an early start. Grandjum and Bridger watch. Molly does, too, fingering the letter she wrote for Lizzie, which she has in the pocket of her jacket, and twisting her hair.

Finally, as the boss loads his sleeping bag and his tent into the backend of the van, she clears her throat. "Dad?"

"Yeah," he says, grunting a little as he bends over to position the tent.

"Can I take a short walk with Doodle? So he'll sleep well on the way home tomorrow?"

The boss gives her an "are-you-kidding?" look. "No." Just then his phone rings.

He stares at the phone, his eyebrows lifted in surprise. "Hey, Matt. What's up?"

He listens as Grandjum and Molly watch him. "Really?" He sounds astonished.

"But you're okay?" He listens a second.

"What happened?" Grandjum asks, eyes wide with concern.

"Hit a deer." The boss mouths, pulling the phone away from his face. "But he's okay." Then, back into the phone, "And your car?" He listens. "We can probably fix that without too much trouble. Where are you?" He listens some more. "Sixteen miles down Big Laurel Creek just past Oak Ridge Drive," he repeats, looking at Grandjum, who nods. "Okay. We'll be there."

He snaps the phone shut. "Came around the corner just past Oak Ridge and a doe just plowed into the side of his SUV. He's okay. The deer is dead. His car has a broken turn light."

"So we got our deer after all," Grandjum exclaims. "I'll get the truck."

The boss runs into the house to explain things to Marmie, who follows him back outside. Then he jumps in beside Grandjum. Soon the truck disappears in a cloud of dust.

"How long do you think they'll be gone?" Molly asks Marmie.

"Oh, probably at least an hour. Maybe two. It's a curvy road to get there, and then they have to load the deer and tie it down."

Molly suddenly looks cheerful. "Think I'll take Doodle for a short walk then." She grabs my leash from the van.

Huh? I thought the boss said no. But Marmie, who was inside at the time, merely says, "By yourself, right? Not to Lizzie's?"

Molly shakes her head, the innocence on her face at odds with the stringy quality to her voice. "No, not to Lizzie's. I promise."

Marmie smiles. "Okay. Keep to the roads and wear your orange vest."

So, once again we suit up and we're off. Molly jogs most of the way there, stopping sometimes to get her breath. She keeps me on leash the whole time. The sun shines with more warmth than we've had in days, and when we get to the little pool, I think I'd particularly enjoy lapping the icy cold water.

But Molly heads straight for the tree and shoves the envelope down under the leaves. "I hope she's able to get here before spring," she says. "Her dad is probably watching her like a hawk. I wish there was a way we could prove Zeke's a liar."

I give the leash a tug towards the pool and Molly says, "Okay, you can get a drink." While I lap, she studies the terrain. "Zeke came from that direction." She points toward a thicket of laurels that climbs a hill.

She pulls out her phone. "We've been gone twelve minutes. Takes maybe nine to get back from here. So if we don't go longer than ten minutes from here we can be back before Dad."

I'm game. These woods have a whole buffet of scents I'd like to sample. She leads me back and forth, like a dog casting for a scent only she's using her eyes instead of her nose. And then says in surprise, "Look at that. A trail."

We follow it to the top of a hill. Now, in addition to all the earthy-leafy scents, I detect another, a faint one of wood smoke and possibly something cooking. Hard to tell exactly where it comes from, though. It would be easier going for both of us if I were off-leash, but Molly keeps it attached even though we have to stop occasionally for her to untangle it, which for some reason she blames on me.

The trail runs down the hill, sometimes curving around giant laurel bushes, and then back up again. Deer use this route—quite frequently by the number of droppings my nose detects along the path.

We work our way down and then over another ridge to yet another little valley, Molly often bending to get under some of the tall laurels. From here, we can see a long rise that ends in a rocky outcropping. Molly stops and checks her phone. "Seven and a half minutes to here," she says. Then, "Oh, Doodle, what have you done?"

I don't think it's my fault exactly that the leash has become tangled around some particularly grasping blackberry vines. She tries to free it, then glances at her phone again and unclips the leash from my collar. "We'll get it on the way back."

The smell from the fire is stronger now and I sniff deeply, examining it. No food that I can detect, but something sharper.

We climb the slope. Just before we reach the top, Molly stops again and whispers, "Do you smell that?" As if she needs to ask! Always behind in the scent-detecting, humans are. She steps cautiously up to the jutting rock and peers around it. She jumps back. "Too visible," she says under her breath. She yanks off her vest, and my scarf, shoving them in some leaves under a laurel.

Edging up to the rock, she peeks over it and I stick my head over to see as well. Now I know where the scent of smoke comes from. At the bottom of this ridge, near the stream, a fire burns under a big round tank of some kind. Several men stand beside it, talking in low voices.

"Is that...?" Molly asks under her breath. Molly takes out her camera and fidgets with it, then looks through it. "Zeke!" she mouths.

I see three men and one of them has a white beard, but, to be honest, I can't say I recognize any of them through the bundle of jackets and hats. One of them carries a rifle slung over one shoulder. But then a gust of wind wafts the scents past us. Zeke it is—the bad Zeke—along with two men I've never met. And, uh-oh. Another scent I'd know anywhere. Rocky.

Molly starts clicking her camera, pointing it this way and that as she snaps photos. "What's that thing on the fire?" she whispers at one point. "What are they doing?"

Don't know. I'm more worried about Rocky.

And then Molly breathes, "Rats. Card's full." She sits with her back to the outcropping, pops open a little compartment in her camera and pulls out a small black object. Then she zips open her camera case.

But I'm on the alert. Do I hear something? I cock my head and listen. A rustling through the leaves. And then I see movement, emerging from one of the bushes on the hillside below. Rocky.

Molly, still bent over her camera, shows no sign of hearing him.

I let forth with a volley of barks to warn her.

Molly gasps. "Doodle! Shut-up!" She sounds scared.

As well she might be, because Rocky bolts forward, barking up a storm, heading straight toward us. The men raise their heads and start to run after the dog.

Molly peeks around the edge of the rock. I bark several times to let Rocky know I see him.

"Oh, no." It comes out half whisper, half wail. She shoves her camera in her pocket. Bending low, she starts to run back in the direction we came, but then turns and runs straight for a thicket of laurels. Rocky bounds over the crest of the hill. He stops, then races toward Molly's retreating form.

Can't let that happen. With a single bark, I charge him, making a feint toward his flank.

He spins and snaps at me, his teeth clicking on air. I spring at him again, lightly biting his shoulder as his teeth make contact with the fur on my neck. I pull back but just barely out of reach. He lunges and I leap away, into a mat of laurels that break my escape and bounce me forward. Rocky's teeth rip through the edge of my ear.

With a yowl of pain, I bite back, but only get a mouthful of hair. I twist out of reach and race into the woods, leading him away from Molly, leaping over branches and old logs, Rocky in hot pursuit.

I concentrate on staying just far enough ahead so that he doesn't give up the chase. Or catch me. He's fast, but I'm faster—he's got that whole overweight thing slowing him down. Plus, he wastes a lot of energy barking.

Behind us, I hear shouts and curses from the other men, who have finally come over the ridge. I run down a hill and up another, the men disappearing from sight. Finally Rocky begins to slow and then he stops altogether, panting hard, his head down, his tongue almost to the ground.

To be honest, I'm pretty tired myself. I plop down onto the leaves in a spot where I can keep my eye on him. Drops of blood drip from the ear that Rocky tore and I discover a small gash in my side I hadn't noticed. I lick it when I can catch my breath enough between pants.

"Rocky!" Zeke's voice comes from beyond the ridge. "Rooooo—cky! Come!"

This goes on for some time, while Rocky just stands, head low, sides heaving. Finally, he looks up in the direction of Zeke's voice and, with frequent hostile glances towards me, trots toward the voice.

I stay where I am, listening.

"There you are! Come! What's wrong with you?" The anger in Zeke's voice would make any dog want to run away rather than come, but then Zeke shouts, "Got him. Any sign of that other dog?"

One of the men says something I don't quite understand.

"I don't like it," Zeke says. "That dog's usually with the Hunter girl. You see any sign of her?"

Molly. In the heat of the fight with Rocky, I'd forgotten about her. I stand and raise my head, sniffing, but don't catch her scent.

"Nothing," comes an answer.

"I don't like it," Zeke repeats. "She might've been with the dog. Could have seen something. Damn interferin' kid. I told her flat out to stay out of these woods. Her and Lizzie's always up to something."

He huffs some of his words, and I can hear the soft thud of footsteps along with occasional crackle of crushed leaves. But they're not coming in my direction.

"You want me to keep watch?" one of the men asks. He has a low wheezy voice that I associate with smokers. Vile stuff, cigarettes, and eating one can make you *really* sick. Just sayin'.

"Guess so. Till we finish this batch, anyways. Then we'll break it up case anyone comes a'looking. Jimmy, you start loadin' the truck."

Now that I remember Molly, I badly want to find her. But I don't think it's a good idea to let these men know I'm here and I certainly don't want to remind Rocky of my presence. I give the gash in my side a few more licks. It's not that deep, but even so I feel it when I move.

I slink cautiously down the hill, keeping to the laurels, moving in a wide arc, so that when I finally come to where I can see the trail again, I'm quite a distance below the ridge outcropping where Molly ran into the trees. I hide inside a laurel. Good thing, too. At the top of the ridge, right where Molly took pictures, a man sits, his back against the stone. I lie down and watch and, after a while, nap fitfully, waiting for him to leave.

Voices wake me up. That, and the sound of a truck starting. It's not dark, but the whole area is in deep shadow. The man is gone from the ridge. I steal across the trail and into the cover on the other side. Now I have work to do. I test the air searching for Molly's scent. I pick up traces of it, but nothing to give me a sense of direction.

A door slams, and after a squeal of brakes, the engine gets first louder, and then fades. I go back up the trail, casting about for the strongest part of Molly's scent. I find the place where she left the trail and follow it through a thicket of laurels, over a fallen log, and then up and over a small rise. On the other side, the scent ends. I sniff in ever-widening circles.

"Doodle!"

Molly's whisper startles me. I move toward it, sniffing like crazy.

"Up here," she says, just as I hone into her scent. I follow it, nose to the ground right into the rough bark of a—

"Up here!"

I look up, and there she is, sitting in the fork of two large branches. I jump up, paws on the tree, wagging my tail. She scoots down along the trunk and lands with a soft thud onto a wide patch of moss along the base of the tree.

"Shhh," she says in a severe whisper.

Oh. Guess I whined. And somehow, I'm licking her face.

She runs her hands down my side. "What's this?" She sucks in her breath as she fingers the gash in my side and then my torn ear. "I hate Rocky. And Zeke." Then she sees my ear. "Oh, Doodle," she says softly. "If you hadn't drawn him away, he would have gotten me for sure."

We exchange hugs—on her part—and licks—on mine—and then she stands up and brushes herself off. She pulls out her phone. "Four-forty-eight," she says. "I tried to call Dad from the tree, but there's no signal here. I've got to find one. He's going to kill me. And I dropped my SD card. I've got to find it. Then at least Dad'll know Zeke's bad and a liar."

She shivers with a backward glance at the tree. "It was cold up there." She takes off at a brisk walk. "Hurry. We have to find the trail. We only have a half an hour at the most before dark."

Are we going back to the trail or somewhere new? Because she takes off in the wrong direction. I hesitate.

"Come *on,* Doodle. We have to hurry." She waves an arm at me. "I'm going to be on restriction for the next *three* Christmases."

I catch up to her. Guess we're going somewhere new. We trudge up one hill and down another, crackling through the leaves under the trees. At the top of the second hill, Molly stops and stares out despondently. "Where's the trail? I was sure it'd be here."

I'm not sure why she'd think that, since it's obviously behind us. I whine and turn so my head is facing the direction of the trail. Usually Molly's good at figuring out what I mean—at least, better than most humans—but she just sighs and takes out her phone.

"No signal," she says. Hey, what's with her voice? She sounds as if she's ready to cry. "What are we going to do now?"

Chapter 10

Lost

I T'S ALMOST DARK," SHE SAYS, HER VOICE EDGED WITH
fear. "Where *is* it?"

Not sure if she means the trail or Marmie's place or her lost
SD card or maybe none of those since we continue in the same
direction away from them all.

We work our way down the ridge, through a nasty section
of wild raspberry vines that gouge us with every step and then
over another ridge and down again. Molly checks her phone
every few minutes. "I wonder if I should turn it off," she says
at one point. "To save the battery." She stands staring at it for a
minute, takes a shaky breath—the kind that means she's close
to tears—and then shoves it back into her pocket. "If we could
just find the *trail*. If I had a smart phone, I'd have GPS."

No clue what she's talking about, but if she wants to go home,
I can help. I turn towards the trail and Marmie's and take a few
steps. I'm usually good for any length walk, but frankly I'm
ready to be back at Marmie's, sacking out with Bridger. I can
almost see the house, the yellow light on the porch, almost
smell turkey leftovers. My stomach tells me it's past dinner

time and even kibble is sounding delicious right now. And the breeze, which was chilly earlier, has turned cold.

"Come on, Doodle," Molly says, still heading in the wrong direction. I whine.

"I know," she says, her voice breaking. "I want to be home, too. And I don't think we're going to make it before dark."

Probably not, since the trees now look like long black shadows against a charcoal sky. We trudge up and down a few more hills, until, at the top of a ridge, Molly stiffens, then inhales sharply. "What's that?" She stares. "Car lights. There's a road over there. How many ridges away is that?"

Can't answer except the lights aren't close. We watch them slowly wind out of sight.

Molly sighs and swallows. "We've got to keep going." And so we continue as the darkness deepens, until Molly trips over a branch and sprawls down onto a mat of leaves. For a moment, she doesn't move and I sniff her face to see if she's hurt. She sits up and wraps her arms around my neck. "Oh, Doodle, what are we going to *do*?" She starts to cry, and for a long time, I stand still while she sobs into my fur. Finally, she releases me, wipes her eyes with the sleeve of her jacket and pulls out a tissue from the pocket to wipe her nose. She takes a deep breath and then another.

"I guess we're here for the night," she says. "So we better be smart about it." She takes a tentative step, hits a branch and steps back. "If I ever go anywhere in the woods again, I'm taking a flashlight," she mutters. And then, "Hey!" She pulls out her phone and holds it away from her. It casts a thin light that she moves around. "Only twenty percent," a cryptic remark—"so I can't do it very long."

Using her phone as a light, she works her way to the base of a large tree.

"Leaves," she says, another puzzler, until she begins scooping leaves into a pile at the tree base. She scans the ground quickly with the phone, then gathers the leaves in the dark. "Ouch!" She tosses a branch out from her armful of leaves. "At least we don't have to worry about poison ivy. Or spiders." After another armful, she adds, "I hope." And then, after another, "*Ticks!*"

Ticks don't bother me, or fleas, because, as I might have mentioned before, I take meds that keep them away. I don't think Molly does, though.

While she scoops, I sniff out our area and mark a perimeter, just to let any potential intruders know this is our territory and make sure there's nothing to worry about. I don't find anything that smells like a threat. At one end, I smell a mouse, which sounds like a mighty good snack right now, but I'm not able to find it.

When Molly has a good-sized mound at the tree base, she burrows into it, sitting with her back to the trunk. She calls for me to join her. "Down," she says, so I lie down against Molly, who pushes leaves over her legs and mine—although I don't really need it, since I have my winter coat—and then rests her head on my neck.

"Oh, my phone." She digs out the phone, and then turns it off. "So it won't be dead in the morning," she says. She repositions herself back under the leaves.

"At least you're here with me," she says, snuggling against my fur. "I don't know what I'd do otherwise. Tomorrow, we'll make it to the road. So, I guess this is good night."

But I'm afraid it doesn't turn out to be a good night, after all. Molly takes forever to get to sleep, twitching and re-adjusting her head right as I start to doze. And then, after her breathing finally becomes slow and regular and I drift off, we're both awakened by an ear-piercing screech that has me up and barking before I remember Molly's half on top of me.

"What was that?" she whispers. I can smell her fear. I bark some more, then check out the area around us. She turns on her phone and shines the light in an arc that shows us nothing and doesn't come near the source of the sound. I can't catch a scent of anything either. I patrol the area for some time before returning to Molly.

"Maybe a screech owl," she says. "I hope."

We burrow again under the leaves. Molly's heart beats fast and hard, but after a long time it finally slows down. I drift off again.

I awake to the sound of coyotes yipping—always something that makes a dog both nervous and somehow envious. The moon shines between puffs of white clouds, and the trees now look like silvery stalks reaching to the deep nothingness of the sky. A light frost covers the leaves, sparkling like tiny stars under the moonlight. I raise my head and listen to the coyotes, tempted to answer them with a long, soulful howl of my own, but know that wouldn't be a good idea. When I'm satisfied that they're too far away to do us harm, I go back to sleep.

By dawn, I have to admit that even with my winter coat I'm glad for Molly's warmth on my side and for our little blanket of leaves on the other. I can see my breath and the frost that sparkled in the moonlight now lies in a delicate pattern over the ground. I'm stiff and want to get up, but don't move until Molly stirs.

"Brrr," she says in a thick voice, when she finally wakes up, her teeth chattering. She pulls out her phone, but then shoves it back into her pocket. "We'll wait till we're higher." She stands, brushes off the leaves, and then takes off at a brisk pace, not slowing down until we reach the top of the next ridge, where she stops to check her phone.

"Only thirteen percent," she says grimly. "And a half a bar." She studies the screen. "Dad's called 15 times. And—" she sounds amazed—"*Mom* called five times. And I have seven texts from Tanya. And Annie called twice." She presses a key eagerly, watches the screen, and then scrunches her eyes. "Not strong enough to connect." The intense discouragement in her voice makes me lick her hand. She swallows hard. "Maybe we'll get it at the road."

We pretty much follow a pattern: down the hill to the bottom, back up to the next one, except that after a few—how many I can't be sure—Molly exclaims, "There it is!" and begins to run. She stops at the edge of a narrow asphalt road divided by a broken white line.

She whips out her phone, biting her lip. "Half a bar." She starts running along the road, up hill, her eyes locked on her phone. Just before the crest of the hill, she stops. "Finally!" she breathes, and presses a key. Soon I hear the boss's voice.

"*Molly?*" he asks in an urgent tone.

"*Dad!*"

"Thank God." His voice is thick with emotion. "It's Molly," he shouts out, his voice more distant, as if his head is turned. I hear excited voices in the background. Then, "Are you okay?"

"Yeah. Just got lost. I ... I'm sorry."

"Thank God," he repeats, his voice breaking. "We have half the state looking for you—they spent most of the night searching."

"I'm so sorry." Molly eyes well with tears, which is surprising because I thought she'd be happy to talk to the boss.

"I'm just glad you're safe." Another pause with some snuffling sounds and then a deep breath. "Do you have any idea where you are?"

"We made it to a road. It might be the Parkway 'cause it kind of looks like it. No signs, but there's a dotted line and it's mowed on either side. No shoulder."

"Okay, good. I'll see if they can track you from the cell signal."

"I only have—" Molly pulls the phone from her ear to where she can see it—"eight percent battery left. Should I leave it on?"

"I think so. Hang on a sec—" The sound becomes muffled, but I can hear him talking to someone. "Yeah, leave it on as long as you can. Now—I have a list of questions from the search people. We didn't know where to look at first, and then I remembered that you talked about the creek, and the dogs picked up your scent there. I think they know the direction you took. How long did you walk after that?"

Molly skews her brow as she thinks. "Maybe two hours. Or less. I thought we were going back, but I guess I went the wrong direction."

I'll say. If canine-human communication were better, we'd have been home by supper.

Molly tells the boss about seeing the lights on the road, but how it was too dark to continue and how we spent the night under the leaves.

"That was smart," the boss says. "So Doodle's okay?"

"Yeah, he's fine. He kept me warm all night."

I hear murmuring as if someone is talking to him, and then, in a pinched, unhappy voice, he says, "Hey, Moll, they say I should get off so we don't exhaust your battery. I hate to do it.

It's so good to hear your voice. I was … so … *scared.*" His voice breaks again. "Is that okay?"

"Okay," she says, her voice suddenly deflated.

"Stay right where you are. Don't go anywhere. They're putting patrol cars on the parkway near Marmie's right now and I'm hopping in the van. You'll be okay?"

"Yeah."

"All right. I love you."

Molly snaps shut her phone. "I hope they hurry." She shivers and rubs her hands. Despite the sun warming my fur, the air still has a chill.

For once, what Molly hopes for comes to pass. We don't wait long at all before a police car, lights flashing, cruises into sight and pulls up in front of us. A bulky policeman jumps out. He has thick-soled shiny black shoes, sharply creased tan pants that expand out a bit at the waist, and a blocky, thick-featured face, now fixed in a friendly smile. He smells like cigarette smoke and coffee.

"Molly Hunter?" he asks.

"Yes," Molly says eagerly.

"Thank God." He beams down at her, looking almost as relieved as Molly. "We were mighty worried about you, young lady. You look cold!"

He flips open his trunk and pulls out a thin blanket that he wraps around Molly, then says, "Here, come on into the car. I got the heat on." He opens the passenger door and Molly settles onto the seat gratefully, leaving the door open so I can sit by her side.

The cop goes to the driver's seat and talks into a small microphone. I know about microphones from when we used to visit rest homes in my service dog days. Don't know how they work, but they can make someone's voice ear-shatteringly loud. This one doesn't do that, though.

"I've got her," he says, much like he's talking into a phone, so maybe that's what it is after all. "She looks fine. A little chilled." A voice squawks from the car, kind of like a radio except it's someone talking. The cop tells the person where he is, then puts down the mike.

He gives Molly a reassuring smile. "The EMTs will be here before long and the dispatcher's going to call your father. I bet you're thirsty." He goes back to the trunk and brings her several bottles of water. Molly gulps down most of one, then asks if there's something she can pour some into for me.

The cop shakes his head. "Don't think I have anything…"

So Molly leans out of the car and drips the water so I can lap it. We've done this before on walks. It's not an efficient way to get a drink, but it moistens my tongue.

She pulls out her phone. "I guess it's okay to use up the battery now." She thumbs the keys on her phone, which she calls texting, a kind of communication even harder to understand than phone calls. "Okay, Tanya knows I'm safe."

She turns away from the cop a bit and presses a key. A voice—hey, it's Cori's—comes out of the phone. "Molly! I … um, this is, um, your mother. I hope you're okay. Your dad filled me in with all the stuff about the search and rescue teams. Sounds like they're doing a good job, so hang in there. A whole bunch of people are looking for you. Keep warm. I'm trying to arrange leave to get up there. Keep safe. I … um, I love you."

Molly looks up from her phone, her eyes shining with tears, but her face glowing. "Did you hear that, Doodle?" she says in a soft voice. "Did you *hear* that?"

Of course I did, my hearing being excellent, as I've mentioned before, but I don't know why Molly's so excited about it.

She punches in a number eagerly only to have her face flood with disappointment as her mother's voice comes out from the phone again. "You've reached Cori Vega. Please leave a message."

"Um, this is Molly. Just letting you know I'm okay. My phone is almost dead but I'll try later."

She starts to shut the phone, but it beeps. A huge smile spreads across her face. "Tanya says her whole family is cheering. And her mother says she has a special treat for you, Doodle, 'cause she knows you helped keep me safe." Suddenly Molly leans out from the doorway and hugs me hard. "Which you did."

I hear the whine of the engine before I see the flashing lights of the EMT truck. It pulls to a stop behind the cop car. A stocky woman with a deep tan and close-cropped light colored hair steps out followed by a much thinner, younger man who's a good head shorter. They both are wearing uniforms kind of like the cop's.

"Howdy, Miss Molly," the woman says, with a broad grin as she comes up to us. She reeks of cats, which I'll admit puts me off a bit, but everything about her body language is friendly. "We're sure glad to see you! I'm Vonda, with the Laurel Woods EMT Association and this here is Darren."

Darren grins at Molly and brushes back a swatch of dark curls, which extends almost past his eyes.

"I'm glad to see you, too," Molly answers with some emotion. Then she adds, "I'm … sorry. I … we didn't mean to get lost."

"No one ever does. The important thing is that you're safe." She pats Molly on the shoulder. "Okay, Miss Molly. Let's go get you checked out so you can get back to your daddy and grandparents. They's kind of missing you!"

Molly takes hold of my collar and follows Vonda to a side door in the EMT van.

"Sorry," Darren says, as I start to follow her up the steps. "No dogs inside."

Molly hesitates. "Can we leave the door open? So he can see us?"

"I don't see any problem with that," Vonda says.

"Okay. Doodle, down. Stay."

I lie down, keeping my eyes on her.

Vonda holds a round thing on Molly's chest, then sticks something in her ear.

"Hmm," Vonda says. "Mild hypothermia. And some dehydration. We better get an IV on you and I'm afraid we're going to have to take you to Tri-Area Regional. We'll call your daddy and have him meet you there. Okay?" She gives Molly a reassuring smile.

"What about Doodle?"

I sit up at the sound of my name.

Vonda gives Darren an imploring look. "I'll scrub the van," she says. "Just this once?"

Darren sighs, pushing a lock of hair off his forehead. "Too risky," he says. "Driggers is on today and he'd have us all over the carpet."

A truly baffling statement, and from the look on Molly's face, not just to me.

"Drigger's our boss," Vonda says. "Strictly letter-of-the-law man. We can sometimes transport pets with our patients if we're taking them home, but not to the hospital. They don't have any facilities there to keep animals."

"But my dad will probably be waiting by the time we get there."

"Yeah, but if he ain't there, we'll be in a load of sh—, um, trouble," Darren says.

"We can't just leave him." Molly's voice suddenly is laced with fear. "He's not just a pet. He's a bed-bug detecting dog. Worth lots of money."

Vonda lays a hand lightly on Molly's arm. "Honey, we wouldn't leave him even if he was just a pet—we know he's part of your family. What we'll do is have Roy over there—" she tilts her head toward the cop who's standing beside his car smoking—"Officer McClone, keep him until Animal Control comes and gets him."

"Animal Control?" Molly says with alarm. "Like the pound?"

"Well, yes—but not in this case. I'll call them and have them take the dog—is it Doodle?—take him to your grandparents' place. Would that be okay?"

"I guess." Molly gives me a worried look.

Darren takes out his phone. "I'll make sure they know he's no stray. And Roy will, too." He makes several calls while Vonda sticks something into Molly's arm that connects her to a long tube. Then he goes over and talks with the cop.

"Okay," Darren says when he returns. "All set."

Molly frowns, still unhappy. "I don't have a leash. We, um, left it behind."

Darren pushes the hair from his eyes. "No problem. I got something." He comes over to me carrying a short length of rope.

"What's his name?"

"Doodle," Molly says.

"Hey, Doodle, there's a good boy." He attaches the rope to the ring on my collar. "Let's go." He tugs on the rope, leading me toward the cop.

Here's the thing. I don't want to go. I want to be in the van with Molly. I pull back, standing my ground.

"Come on!" Darren gives the rope a jerk.

I don't like this at all. But then Molly says, "Doodle, go. No pull."

I reluctantly follow Darren over to the cop, who takes the rope. "Hey, Bud," he says.

"*Good* boy," Molly says, but she sounds near tears.

Darren goes back and shuts the side door, then hops into the van and then it pulls away.

I whine, watching it go.

The cop leads me to the driver's side of the car. He sits with the door open, holding the rope. He pats me on my head. "It won't be for long. We'll have you home in no time."

Home? Does he mean with Molly? Because that's where home is to me.

Chapter 11

Nabbed

W E WAIT FOR SOME TIME. THE COP CHECKS HIS
watch, sips some coffee from a tall paper cup, waits a
bit longer, and then checks his watch again. "I wonder if they
got lost?"

I barely hear him, because—I stand up and sniff hard. What
is that scent? So familiar, so … irresistible? And then I see
motion across the clearing on the other side of the road, at
the edge of the woods. Turkeys! I *love* turkeys—love chas-
ing them, I mean. Nothing more satisfying than when they
all burst into flight with a tremendous noise from their huge
wings. Back in my puppy days, I actually caught a young turkey—ran it down—well, me running, it flying low for a long
distance until it just sort of collapsed and I grabbed it. It says
something about a dog's speed and skill to catch a turkey, and
I was one proud pup that day. But for some reason the bosses
didn't praise me. In fact, they took it from me the first chance
they got.

The cop's radio squawks and I kind of hear something about
an accident, but I'm not really listening.

106 👻 Susan J. Kroupa

Because just then the turkeys, maybe spooked by the radio, bolt along the tree line in long-legged strides. Without thinking, I leap forward to give chase. The rope jerks from the cop's hand. He curses and jumps out of the car. "Doodle! Come. *Come!*"

I will, I will. In just a little bit. But right now, I'm reveling in the sheer joy of running. My legs fly over the grass. My paws thrust me forward in quick, satisfying thuds, the hot scent of live turkeys filling my nose. I close the distance between me and the flock. They take off in earnest now and just as I'm coming up on them, a bunch of them flush into the sky. But one of them, a juvenile maybe half-grown, keeps running. I'm gaining on it, closer and closer. I snap at its tail feathers and one breaks loose.

Now it flaps its wings in a desperate effort and rises off the ground, flapping hard. If it flew up to a tree limb, it'd all be over, and it would be laughing at me. But, just like in my puppy days, it doesn't. It flies just high enough that I can't quite grab it from the air. I push my legs harder and try a little leap, but that just puts me further behind. I redouble my efforts and once again close the gap. And then—is this wonderful or what?—*just* like before, the turkey falls to the ground. I snatch it in a flash, and shake it hard several times. It doesn't move, but droops limp and lifeless in my mouth.

I drop it, then, panting hard. Every muscle in my body trembles from the effort and for awhile I can't seem to get enough air. I settle down beside it until my panting eases up. Suddenly, I remember Molly. And the cop. It's time to be getting back.

I pick up the turkey, delighting in the way its scent pools in my nostrils, and trot back toward the road. Unlike Molly,

I have a good sense of direction and soon I hear the cop's voice calling. "Doodle! Doodle!" And another man's voice as well, one I don't know.

They both sound angry so I draw closer cautiously. They're a little ways into the woods, some distance from each other. They each call my name, turning from side to side, searching. But nothing about their body language indicates that it would be good to go to them. Especially the cop. He sounds seriously ticked off.

I remember how the bosses took my turkey when I was a pup. I lie down in a laurel bush where I can watch from safety.

Finally, the cop uses a few words that the boss would call "language" and says, "He's gone. How am I going to tell that to the kid?" He sighs and walks with heavy steps back toward the clearing, and the other man joins him. I follow from a distance, carrying my turkey, and watch as the cop goes to his car and the man to a white van with bars in the windows parked behind it. Both drive away.

I go to the road and drop the turkey in order to sniff things out. The scent of the cop and his car suddenly remind me that we were waiting for someone to take me home. And then I think, *Molly*, and suddenly feel very alone.

I settle down with my turkey to wait. After a bit, I get up and sniff the ground, where the EMT truck was. Its scent is overlaid with the fresher odors from the white van, which strangely enough smells like dogs and cats along with the typical engine and gasoline scents. I catch a whiff of Molly's scent, very faint, but distinct.

I'm thinking that maybe I should follow the EMT van to wherever it took Molly. I don't think she's coming back. I'd have to leave the turkey to do so—the turkey's scent would override everything else. It's a tough decision. Finally, I find a soft spot in the earth and spend some time digging a shallow hole where I bury the turkey so it'll be safely there if I return.

I go back to where the EMT was parked and hone in on its particular scent. I excel at what some trainers call nose work, of course, being an expert in bed bug detection. Even so, I find it tough to follow. I cast back and forth and work my way down the road, nose to the ground.

And then I hear the sound of an engine. I lift my head, ears forward.

Not the boss's van. I know that before the old gray pickup rattles into sight. Still I stand, watching it. Could this be what the cop was waiting for?

Two men crane their necks at me as the pickup passes me. It slows at the top of the hill, then turns around and comes back. This time, the truck stops alongside me.

"Looky that," says the driver, a pimply teenager so thin that his nose and Adam's apple look oversized for his face. "One of them fancy dogs. Labdoodles or somethin'. They's worth lots of money. My cousin down in Charlotte bought one for like two grand. Was gonna breed it and make lots of money, but then it got out and got hit by a car."

He leans out the window and studies me. I stare back at him, curious.

"Male," he says in a disappointed voice. "But they's still worth lots."

"I dunno," the other man says. He's older, but not by much, and just as thin, with a short scar on one cheek and a scraggly goatee—which I learned early on has nothing to do with goats.

"Like we're in with designer dog folks. Now, if he was a pit, he could fight."

"Waste of money to fight him," the teen says. "Too puny, and anyways worth way more than that."

"Where we gonna find a buyer? And we'd have to feed it and all."

"Larry might take him, over in Sparta. He has a friend who runs a pet store who takes dogs no questions asked if they's worth somethin'. Larry's hunted up dogs for him before. Fancy breed pets people leave out in their yard. Good money innit."

"I guess," the older man says. "All right. You git 'em."

I take a few steps backward as the door to the truck opens with a screech like a cat in pain and the pimply man steps out. "Here, doggy. Come on, boy." He gives me a grin that shows several half-decayed teeth. He has a bad smell, too, pungent, like cleaning chemicals. I take a few more steps back.

"Okay." He narrows his eyes in a way that doesn't inspire confidence. He goes back to the truck and returns with a rope and something else in his hand.

"Hey, boy, look't what I got here. Burger."

"You ain't gonna give him my extra, is you?" the goatee man protests.

Burger. I sniff and catch the scent and start to drool. It smells really good and it's been a long time since I've eaten. I take a few steps forward.

"That's a good boy. Come on." He stretches out a yellow-nailed hand smudged with dirt and grease. A hand that holds a hamburger.

I reach for it, but just as I open my mouth, he pulls it back.

I stop, a line of drool dangling almost to the ground.

"Come on. All the way."

I step forward and this time he gives it to me, but grabs the rope dangling from my collar. Normally, I chew my food but this time I swallow it in a couple of gulps. A bird in the hand, as the boss would say, which, it turns out, has nothing to do with birds, but means if you think someone might take away your food, you'd better swallow it quick.

"Got 'im," pimply man says, pulling me forward and taking hold of my collar.

I try to pull away, but he holds me with a firm grip. Suddenly, I don't like him at all. I twist and pull as he yells at goatee man while holding me with both hands. I growl and bare my teeth. I'm not the kind who bites humans, but I'm starting to think this man might change that. Except I can't seem to reach him. He's worked his way behind me and holds me from behind.

Goatee man runs up and the next thing I know I have a noose around my neck and he's pulling it so tight I can hardly breathe. I paw at the rope and try to snap at it, but again make no contact. And then I'm being dragged by the two men over to the back of the pickup. I gasp and cough, trying to get some air, but nothing works and I start to black out as they lift me and drop me into the back. I feel rather than see thick fingers working the rope around my neck, loosening it until I'm able to grab a big gasp of air. I begin to pant furiously, trying to restore the air to my lungs. I look up to see goatee man fling my collar over the side of the truck.

"Jest another lost dog," he says, his grin showcasing his mouth of bad teeth.

I hear the doors slam and the next thing I know the truck takes off down the road. Time to get out of here. I rise, lurching under the motion of the truck, and still panting hard even though it's cold. But when I pull away, something yanks my head back. The rope is tied to a rail that runs along the inside of the truck. I try to twist loose of the rope, but only succeed in pulling it tighter around my neck. The truck picks up speed and the air rushing past is icy.

I tug a few more times at the rope then reluctantly give up. Nothing to do now but hunker down and wait, wishing I could be back home with Molly and the boss.

Chapter 12

Pet Shop

THE MEN DRIVE FOR A VERY LONG TIME OVER WINDING roads that might have made me sick if it weren't for all the fresh air. Fresh, *freezing* air.

Finally, the truck slows, makes a sharp turn, and then bounces down a narrow bumpy dirt road with more ruts than smooth places. Fortunately, we only go a short distance before pulling up in front of a dirty white trailer with peeling paint fronted with a gray sagging porch. Smoke curls from the chimney, but it has that same peculiar sharpness to the odor as that on the men.

The truck's horn honks in a strange pattern of short and long blasts. The sound makes me jump. A curtain moves in the window of the trailer, and then a man comes out, walking with a slight limp, a shotgun draped over one arm. As skinny as the men in the truck but much older, deep lines score his face and he has a white/gray stubble for a beard. He wears a stained sweatshirt over grease-smeared jeans, topped off with a faded baseball cap that pushes down a mat of stringy gray hair.

"Hey, Nick," he nods at the driver and then turns to the teen. "Chase," he says, with more suspicion than friendliness. He turns his head towards me and narrows his eyes.

"Hey, Larry," says Nick. "Okay we get out?"

The man gives another nod. "What y'all need?"

Nick and Chase get out of the truck. Chase points at me. "We got us one of them ladoodles designer-type dogs. Thought you might trade us for a little stash. They's worth thousands, my cousin Billy says."

"Where'd you git 'im?"

"Standin' on the side of the road, big as life," Chase says proudly. "And I sees him and sez hey that dog's worth somethin'."

Larry walks over to the truck and stares down at me, sucking in one side of his cheek.

"How much y'all askin?"

"A week's supply plus thirty for gas? It's a long way out here."

Larry's eyebrows go up and Nick says quickly, "Twenty'd be okay."

"Ten, and a four-day stash."

Nick looks angry, but he says, "All right."

Larry tilts his head towards the side of the trailer. "Got a cage in my Ford. Let's put him there and I'll run him over to Billy's."

Nick works some chains on the end of the truck, then pulls down the tailgate while Larry gets into a truck as beat up as the one I'm in, and backs it around so the two trucks' tailgates are end to end.

"Let's move him." Larry says. All three men climb into the truck.

Not if I have anything to say about it. I don't like any of these men with their bad teeth and strange odor.

Nick loosens the knot tied to the end of the truck, while Chase holds the part of the rope around my neck. Larry stands off to the side. I'm tempted to growl—but instead I hold still, watching carefully. Nick has a hard time with the knot, but finally tugs the end through the loop. I wait, biding my time, until the knot's completely straight and Nick grabs the end, turning towards me. Chase's hand is on my neck, but his attention is on Nick.

l jump back with all my strength. As I hoped, the rope slides through Nick's fingers. He yelps and comes towards me, cursing. Chase tries to hold me, but I wrench free.

But then Nick slams a boot into my side—the same side that Rocky bit. I reel backwards, and before I can get up, Nick and Chase are on top of me. Did I say I don't bite humans? These two are definitely exceptions, and I'd happily sink my teeth into one of their smelly arms, but Nick sits on my neck and I can't get to them.

"Careful," grunts Larry, "or he won't be worth nothing." The three of them drag me to the other truck and shove me inside a wire crate, much like the one I have in the boss's van, except this smells of other dogs. I lay there, panting, my side throbbing, while Larry gives the other two some money and some small plastic baggies half-filled with a white powder.

Larry's on the phone as soon as Chase and Nick pull away.

"Hey, Billy. Got a dog y'all might want. One of them labdoodles? Someone be there in a hour or so?"

I can't hear what Billy says over the sound of my panting. But Larry says, "Black, maybe 80 pounds. Good condition."

No thanks to them. I lick my side, which still aches from Nick's boot.

"Okay. I'll be there."

Larry goes into the trailer but returns quickly and soon we're bouncing down his road. Nothing for me to do but doze, which I do, until the smell of fast food wakes me up. Reminds me how long it's been since I've had a full meal.

We're in a good-sized town, passing all sorts of restaurants and other businesses. We go through several green lights, and then down a couple of side streets before Larry turns into an alley between two rows of two-story brick buildings. He stops in front of a faded brick, flat-roofed building with sagging gutters and honks the horn in the same pattern that Nick and Chase used.

A stubble-bearded man with a round expanse of belly and hard gray eyes opens the door. He has hair pulled back into a ponytail that reaches almost to his waist. He also has a strong odor. Not the chemical/sharp scent of Nick and Chase, but the one humans get if they haven't bathed in some time. He stares at me for a second. "Looks more standard poodle than labradoodle," he says.

I get that a lot because of my curly coat.

Larry shrugs. "Worth somethin' either way."

The man nods, pulls out his wallet and gives some bills to Larry. Next thing I know, he's reaching into the cage, fitting a pinch collar around my neck. I don't like this and start to pant again.

And then he has a leash on me and opens the door to the crate. He leads me to the edge of the tailgate. "Come on. Get down," he says. I jump to the ground and scratch my ear to relieve a little tension, only to aggravate the cut from Rocky. He waves at Larry, who's already back in the truck and pulling away.

I consider trying to get away, but this man has a firm grip on the leash and I know about pinch collars. He leads me along the side of the building to a weedy spot rich in scents from other dogs. "Come on. Do your business," he says.

Hey, that's what the boss says. This man isn't anything like the boss, though. Still, I'm glad for the chance to lift my leg and relieve myself. Then he leads me back to the door and into the building.

Whoa. A host of scents, mostly animal, hit my nose. We pass a room filled with boxes and stacks of papers and other stuff, into a bigger room with glass windows in front and a cash register on a counter on one side. A large aquarium with brightly colored fish stands near the back wall, while two rows of cages stacked on top of each other fill the wall opposite the cash register. Several small dogs and a couple of fluffy cats occupy the top cages. One of the dogs lets forth with a round of high-pitched barks.

The man pushes me into a cage so small that I can't turn around inside it, and unsnaps the leash but leaves the collar on. I bump my head when I try to sit, so I stand, head low. But the cage has a small bowl of water in it. I drink it all and lick the bowl dry.

The man, meanwhile, has been busy making calls. "Miz Balwick?" he says into the phone. "This is Billy Lee Crawford at Billy's Pet Supplies. Was you the one who was looking for a labradoodle? 'Cause I got one here. His owner died, a sweet old woman, widow, nearly eighty. Anyways, her kids don't want to deal with findin' him a home so I took him off their hands." He listens for a bit. "Yeah. Black. Neutered and has all his shots. In great condition. I think the family said he was four." More listening. "$450. Which is a great deal for a doodle and it's only $50 profit for me. His owners paid two grand for him as a pup. Great bloodlines, they say. Australian labradoodle." He nods while making a note on a slip of paper by the register. "Yeah. Okay. Remember cash only. Yeah, talk to your husband. Just to let y'all know, I got a few others says they's interested. First one through the door with the money gets him."

He makes a few more calls saying pretty much the same thing. Then he spends time on a laptop.

I take a nap since there's nothing else to do. A bell on the door awakens me and sets the small dog into a flurry of barking. The sun slants in through the windows at a low angle. I check my water dish, but it's still empty.

A woman bursts into the room who somehow reminds me of a walking stick—the insect, I mean—tanned brown, all gangly with short hair that sticks straight up on top, thin lips, and round bug-like eyes. She's so thin she looks as if she hasn't had a decent meal in some time. "Sorry, it's so close to closing. I had to go to the bank." She turns toward me, pointing.

"That him?" She marches over to my cage and stretches out a brown, knobby-knuckled hand to touch the top of my head. I'd move away if I could, but I can't.

"Hey, boy, how you doing? You're beautiful!" She turns to the man who has left his laptop to come stand beside her. "What's his name?"

The man hesitates for a fraction of a second, before he says with a little bluster, "Max. But people rename dogs all the time. They's smart, these labradoodles. It don't take them long to learn new things. You could call him anything you like."

"Hey, Max," the woman coos. "How you doing, boy?"

Seriously? How does she think I'm doing trapped in a too-small cage without enough water with people I'd just as soon not be around? I lay my head down, not looking at her. She has a nervous energy that makes me want to scratch, and her scent is laced with tension.

"I think he's missin' his folks," the man says, "so he's sort of reserved-like."

"Yeah," the woman says with authority. "Labradoodles can be that way. Takes them awhile to bond, but then they're great dogs." She pats my head a few more times. "Can I take him out of the cage?"

"Sure thing." The man attaches a leash and opens the gate. I hurry out into the room, grateful for the chance to stretch and to scratch my ear.

The woman leads me in circles around the inside of the store. "Sit," she says at one point. I sit. "Down." I lie down. "Kind of dirty," she observes. "But seems well-enough trained."

"The family that had him took him to obedience school. Said he was the smartest dog in the class."

I think about Miguel and my training with him. I don't remember him ever saying I was the smartest dog—although it certainly could be true. But Miguel had a way of making every dog feel like the smartest dog while in training. He was good that way.

The woman pats me on the head again and doesn't seem to notice when I melt back from her touch. She straightens up. "Four fifty?"

"Cash and no returns. I got three other's comin' to see him. If he don't work out, you can sell him yerself. I'll throw in the collar."

The woman nods. "Okay. I'll take him." She squats down and strokes my chest. "Hey, Max, I'm Kristin. You're going to come live with me now. I know you miss your family, but I'm going to give you a forever home."

Not sure what she means by forever home, but she's right about missing my family.

The man puts me back in my cage while the woman pays him and picks out an assortment of other items. Then, once again a leash is attached, a new leather one, and the woman leads me outside, while the man hefts a big bag of dog food that he drops into the back seat of an SUV.

Kristin lifts up the end door. "Up you go." She pats the rubber mat in the cargo space, tugging the leash at the same time. "Hop in."

I hop in reluctantly. Pinch collar, remember? At least I have room to sit without bumping my head. A net stretches across the top rim of the back seat, blocking the cargo area from the rest of the car. Kristin shuts me in and then gets in the driver's seat.

And then we're on the road once again. Frankly, I'm getting sick of traveling, and I don't just mean that I'm queasy, which I am, but that I'm tired of it.

We pass through town and then alongside the rolling pastures and woods beyond town that look much like the area where Marmie and Grandjum live. I keep watch, hoping maybe to see their house, although somehow I suspect it can't be this close.

Just when I'm about to lie down and take a nap, we turn onto a smooth gravel road that winds to the top of a hill and into the driveway of a small log house with a neat yard. Big pots of mums, the blooms mostly dead, sit on either side of steps leading up to a narrow porch supported by fat logs. Several other planters jut out from the posts, and a row of trimmed bushes lines the base of the porch.

A garage door opens right as we come up to it, and closes again as soon as we're inside. I've seen doors do this before, and am no longer freaked out by it, although I've never quite understood how they work.

"Here we are," Kristin says brightly. "Your new home!" But she doesn't immediately get me out of the SUV. Instead, she disappears through a door, returning shortly with a hawk-nosed man, bald except for a fringe of hair around his ears, as thin and brown as she is.

"Max, meet Paul," Kristin says, opening the backend at last. She clips on the leash.

Paul stares at me without enthusiasm. "Awfully big."

"Not for a labradoodle. Some weigh over a hundred pounds."

Paul's mouth curls downward as if this isn't especially good news. I'm aware suddenly of a tension between them. They don't seem to like each other much, these two.

Kristin leads me through the side door, into a wood paneled kitchen with shiny, varnished floors. A rich aroma of beans cooking with tomatoes fills the room, from an electric pot on the counter, along with a smoky scent of cinnamon and vanilla that seems to come from two fat candles burning on the window sill.

My nails click on the floor and Paul gives me a disapproving look.

"I'll get them trimmed," Kristin says tersely.

She leads me past a small table with a brightly patterned tablecloth and two rustic looking chairs through a door on the opposite side, which opens to a patch of grass surrounded by a chain-link fence. The fence is puny compared to the one around the boss's yard, which is good news. Let's just say that one gave me no problem getting over and this looks even easier. Except Kristin still has the leash connected to the prong collar around my neck.

The yard itself is no bigger than the boss's yard in Arlington, which is strange because the closest house is one ridge over. You can see for quite a ways in every direction from here. I look out over the rolling hills. The sun has set and the broad clusters of trees look black against the sky.

Kristin shivers. With the sun gone, the air has turned cold. "Hurry up, Max. Pee."

She walks me around the perimeter of the fence, where I take in all the local scents. No other dogs as far as I can smell, nor cats. I pee a few times—best to establish my presence while I have the chance—and Kristin says, "Good boy," as if I've done something remarkable.

We go back into the kitchen. "Let's get that thing off of you," Kristin says. She unhooks the prong collar and rubs my neck, which I admit feels good. Never been a fan of prong collars myself. The service dog people never used them, but my second boss, the one I don't like to remember, used to jerk me around quite a bit with one. Sometimes I'd get sores on my neck that lasted for weeks.

Miguel didn't like to use them either, although he taught the boss the correct way to attach and use them, because the boss felt I was too powerful for Molly to walk otherwise. And Molly never hurt me except to give me a momentary little jerk if I was pulling too hard. *Molly*! Thinking of her makes something ache deep in my chest.

Kristin puts on a new collar, a fabric one that snaps together. "That better?" she asks. She gives me a pat on the head, then goes to the garage, returning with the sack of dog food on her shoulder.

Okay. Got my interest.

She takes a bowl from the bag of items she bought at the pet store and puts some of the dog food in it. I've always loved the rattle that kibble makes as it's being poured into a dish. I remember that it's been a long time since I've had any kind of meal.

But before she gives me the bowl, she opens a can of meaty-smelling stuff, and scoops some on top of the kibble. I'm liking this Kristin better all the time, even if she does pat me on the head.

She sets it down for me in one corner of the kitchen. I take a bite. Delicious! The meaty stuff tastes wonderful and even the kibble tastes better than usual. I don't think it's just because I'm so very hungry, but either way, I enjoy every morsel and lick the bowl clean. While I'm eating, Kristin places a metal bowl filled with water beside my dish. So, I finish my meal with a nice drink.

"Water might stain the floor." Paul has come into the kitchen and is filling a small bowl with some of the stew in the pot.

"I'll get a mat to put under it," Kristin sounds irritated. She's carrying a rug she got from the garage. She puts it against the wall near my food and water dishes. "This will have to do until we can get you a dog bed," she says. I curl down onto it, very sleepy now that I finally have a full stomach.

I nap while they eat dinner, and then, after another trip out to the yard, I nap on a throw rug by the wood stove in the living room, while Kristin and Paul watch TV. When they click it off, Kristin carries my rug to a room that has a single bed in it.

"You're going to let him sleep in your room?" Paul asks incredulously.

"Not on the bed," Kristin says defensively. "And, anyway, I get lonely." She gives him a look and for a moment her face sags, her eyes brimming with longing. Then she turns and shuts the door.

She places the rug by her bed, then stoops down to pet me. "Oh, Max." Hey, her voice breaks and to my surprise throws her arms around my neck and begins to cry against my fur. I don't quite know what to do, so I stand still until she wipes her eyes, and starts to get ready for bed.

"I'm so glad I found you," she says. "Whatever happens, I know I'll have you."

Chapter 13

Runaway

THE SUN IS LOW ON THE HORIZON THE NEXT MORNING
when Kristin takes me out to the little yard to pee. She
wears a heavy jacket and I can see her breath when she urges
me to hurry up.

After another wonderful breakfast—really, the boss should
find out what kinds of dog food this Kristin gets—she announces
we're going for a walk, which is fine by me. She snaps a pouch
around her waist that has treats, shrugs into her jacket, adds a
hat, and then fits the pinch collar around my neck.

This time we go out through the front door, down the steps
of the porch. I'm taking in brisk air, sorting through all the
early morning scents, when Kristin says, "No pull!" and snaps
the leash causing the collar to bite into my neck. Instinctively,
I jump, causing it to bite harder, and then, suddenly, it shudders under the pressure and drops to the ground.

Kristin gasps and runs towards me. Are we going to play a
game of "chase"? I dodge away.

"Max, come!" She fumbles in the pouch and extracts a treat,
which she holds out in front of her. "Come!" A harsh note of

fear in her voice that tells me she's not playing a game. And then the realization sinks in: I'm free. *Free.*

Molly. Got to get back to Molly. Although I have to admit I'm a bit hazy as to how.

"Come!" Kristin is only an arm's length away. I leap away and start to lope down the driveway.

"Maaaaax!" Kristin wails in real distress.

But I'm already racing towards the thicket of trees at the bottom of the hill, her calls trailing after me.

I run through the woods, down deer paths, jumping over fallen logs, curving around thick laurels, until I come to a field on the other side. I bolt across it, causing more than a few of the cattle grazing there to raise their heads and watch me, ears forward with alarm. I scoot under a barbed wire fence and into the trees on the other side. I keep moving, through woods and fields, over hills and gullies, crossing dirt roads and paved ones and through even more woods and fields. The sun shines bright in a sky dotted with white puffy clouds, the air so clear that everything seems unnaturally sharp. It feels *good* to run, to let all the anxiety from the last few days flow out of me, streaming through my paws into the ground.

When at last I'm too tired to continue, I stop, panting hard. My throat burns with thirst. I put my nose to the air and test the scents. No trace of Kristin. But—I sniff some more and find what I'm seeking—water.

I follow the scent, walking now while my sides heave to catch my breath, through a patch of woods to a muddy stream at the bottom of a small knoll. Just what I needed. I lap and lap and then, still hot, I slop down into the cold, soothing mud. It cakes against my fur. When the cold becomes uncomfortable,

I leave the stream for a dark spot under a bush and curl down to take a rest.

I awake to see the sun setting behind the trees. I get up and shake. A fine layer of mud coats one side of me, and while earlier it cooled me off, now I'm grateful for the extra warmth it gives me. Mud really is a wonderful thing, something humans don't seem to understand. Always rushing a dog to get a bath, just because of a little mud on the fur or paws.

Thinking of baths makes me remember the boss and Molly. Molly! I'd be willing to take a bath just to be back with her again.

My stomach grumbles, which is too bad because I don't smell any food nearby. I think longingly of the great food I had at Kristin's.

Where ever I am, there's a road not too far away. I hear the sound of a car passing, and then, a little later, of a truck. That reminds me of the skinny men with the foul odor. I go back to the creek and take a long drink, add a little more mud to my coat, and then, because my legs are really tired from the day's run, I return to my spot under the bush for another nap.

I awake several times in the night, once to the haunting sound of coyotes. I can't tell if it's the same pack I heard earlier or not, but I snuggle down in my hole, glad they're too far away to be a danger. Another time, the stench—there's really no other word—of a skunk assaults my nose. I lift my head to see one waddling to the creek. I cornered a skunk once in my service dog days. Not a good experience. Let's just say, Lesson Learned. I watch it from my hiding place without moving.

By dawn, I'm rested but hungry. My breath comes out in little clouds at first, but the sun shines in a cloudless sky and soon it starts to warm. I drink from the creek and trot off, keeping my nose alert to the smell of anything edible. I've caught mice before. They like to hide under a layer of leaves, but they can't hide their scent from a nose like mine. But though I stop and search for them in a variety of likely looking spots, I don't smell any.

I keep going until I come to a dirt road. I study it, hoping it might be one of the roads near Marmie's, but it doesn't look at all familiar. I take it, keeping my ears tuned for the sound of a certain pickup or SUV.

I pass a white farmhouse set back from the road with lots of trucks and farm equipment parked by the barn. Horses. Cattle, and chickens by the smell of it. I've heard that some dogs will eat chicken—I mean the live, feathered animals, not the kind the boss cooks—but I've never been interested. At least not since the time I was a pup and tried to chase a hen who gave me a sharp peck on my nose.

Two dogs, border collie mixes, rush from behind the barn and begin to bark, so I trot on past.

Further down the road, I come across a single story house with a garage at one end and a covered porch that runs along the whole front side. Kind of reminds me of Marmie's. No dogs here. Not even a cat.

I start to go on, when the unmistakable aroma of bacon hits my nose. My mouth fills with drool. I follow the scent around to the back of the house to several large windows framed by bright yellow curtains, and, to the side of that, a door.

From inside, I hear the high-pitched voice of a child. "Look'it that dawg." A girl points an arm at me, and then another girl, this one a head taller, comes up beside her.

"Mama, look'it that big dog," the bigger one says, and soon a woman with long dark hair joins them. I move back a little.

"Looks like a giant poodle," she says. "Jacob, come see this."

A man appears beside her. For a moment, no one speaks. They stare out at me and I stare back at them.

"No collar," the woman observes. She shakes her head. "I don't get people who don't put ID tags on their dogs."

"Can we keep it?" the smallest girl asks.

"No," the man and woman both say with some fervor.

"He looks hungry," the smallest girl says. "Look, he's drooling."

Hey, they're right. A line of drool extends down from my mouth. It's been a long time since I've eaten and bacon—well, bacon could make a dog drool who'd just finished a bowlful of food.

"Dogs are always hungry," the man says. "But I suppose we could call the animal shelter and see if anyone's missing him. Don't see many poodles round here."

"You'd think they'd have a collar on him," the woman repeats. She leaves the window and I hear her voice in another room, but can't make out the words.

She comes back shortly. "No one's called in a missing poodle," she says, "but they can come get him by four o'clock today."

The man nods. Pretty soon, the back door opens, and he comes outside.

"Hey, Bud, how you doing?"

I pull back remembering the two foul-smelling men and their vile rope. This man, though, isn't at all like them. He speaks in a quiet, calm voice. And he smells like—well, like bacon, which is pretty irresistible—but also like toast and eggs—also favorites, as well as soap and coffee.

He stops, not coming any closer. "Little bit shy, ain't ya?" He watches me for a few moments and then goes back into the house. I think that maybe I should move on, but frankly the bacon smell kind of has me tethered to this place.

The door opens again and this time the man comes out with the oldest girl. She's thin, with brown hair pulled into two pony-tails in a way that Molly and Tanya sometimes wear. *Molly*, I think, suddenly missing her intensely.

"Hey, boy. You hungry?" She holds out her hand, which has something in it.

I sniff but am too far away to smell it. I come closer, working my nose. I like this girl who kind of reminds me of Molly. No sour smell to her at all.

"I ain't gonna hurt you," the girl says softly. The man standing beside her doesn't move or speak.

I edge a little closer and then I know that she's holding toast. Not bacon, alas. Still, it's food.

"Just want to get you back to your family. Come on."

I move up to her hand, ready to spring back if she grabs at me the way the men did. But she holds still and lets me take the toast, which I gulp down—as I said before, a bird in the hand. Delicious. I run my tongue along the side of my mouth to get any stray crumbs.

Now the mother comes out trailed by the littlest girl, who has light hair that bunches in big curls around her face. "I want to feed him," the girl says.

"Mama, he likes toast," the older girl says. "He's shy. Wonder if someone hit him."

Something like that, I think, remembering the rough hands of the foul-smelling men.

The mother puts a bowl down. "How 'bout some scraps?" She sets it near the door but then steps away from it. I cautiously approach. The dish contains bits of toast, egg, and some scrapings of bacon grease.

After only a moment's hesitation, I go up to it and polish off the contents, licking up every drop of the grease, alert the whole time for any sudden movements from the people. But they all just watch without moving.

"That feel better?" the mother asks softly, when I'm done. "Never fun to be hungry."

Couldn't agree more!

"I'd better get going," the man says. He disappears through the door, and pretty soon I hear the garage door open and a car leave.

"I'll get him some water," the smallest girl says. She comes back a little bit later holding a bowl that sloshes as she walks, and plops it down beside the food bowl.

I just look at it, not being thirsty at this exact moment. I sit, watching all of them, until the girl who reminds me of Molly comes over to me. This time I don't pull away. She pets my back in long, smooth strokes. "He's so curly," she says.

"Like he's got a perm," her sister says.

Pretty soon her little sister joins her, and for some time they pet me and talk to me. No one tries to tie me up. In fact, it feels good to have the girls' attention, even though none of these people will replace Molly. Or the boss, now that I think about it. For all that he's sometimes stern and tends to look on the pessimistic side of things, he's always been a good boss.

The two girls stay outside with me most of the day. After lunch, they give me the crusts from their sandwiches, which I welcome, and later on the youngest feeds me a few crackers.

When the shadows from the trees lengthen and the air starts to get a chill, a van pulls up in the driveway. A heavy-set, well-muscled man, wearing black boots and a faded gray uniform steps out. He has black button eyes set in a round face and reminds me a bit of the cop that helped Molly. Before he can make it to the front door, it opens and the mother hurries out, flanked by the two girls.

"He's over there," the mother says, pointing at me.

"Don't see many of those," the man says. "Poodle!"

Another common mistake, since, as my first boss used to say, I'm "much more doodle than labra." Which I think is how I got my name.

The man continues to regard me. "Somebody'll be missing him, I'll bet on it." He opens the back door of his van and comes out with a leash.

I watch warily, wondering what he's doing.

But then, the girls run over to me and throw their arms around my neck. "He's a nice dawg," the littlest one says. And the next thing I know, the man is beside them and he's slipped the leash around my neck. I pull back, but he's strong and doesn't budge.

"Hey, boy, I won't hurt ya," the man says in a voice that somehow calms me. "We're going to take you somewhere safe."

"Bye, now," says the girl with hair like Molly's. Her voice shakes a little. "You be a good dog."

The youngest girl begins to cry. "Cain't we keep him? He's really, *really* nice."

"Hush, Savannah," the mother says. "I already told y'all we can't."

"But what if no one claims him?" the older girl asks. "We cain't let them put him down. He's a *good* dog."

The mother sighs. She turns to the man. "How much time does he get, before…"

"I think four of five days, ma'am. More if he had a collar."

The mother frowns. "Could you let us know? If none of his people come get him?"

The youngest girl says, "Yay! We could name him Curly."

"I'm *not* saying we'd keep him," the mother says firmly. "We don't have a fenced yard and I think it's just plain mean to keep a dog chained up. Just that we'd try to find him a good home."

The man nods. "Yes, ma'am. I can't do it myself, but you could call over to the shelter and give them your name and such. Let them know you're interested if no one comes."

The man starts to tug me towards the van. I quit pulling and follow him since I don't seem to have a choice. He leads me to a crate just inside the door. I jump back, reluctant to go into it, but he pushes from behind, pulling forward at the same time, and before I know it I'm inside.

As he shuts the door to the van, I hear the youngest girl cry, "Bye, Curly. We love you."

I'm not sure how long the van drives because, as usual on car rides, I take a nap. We finally stop in front of a long thin brick building. Its mildly slanted roof overhangs a cement walkway running the length of each side. Narrow strips of brown grass flank the cement walkways. The whole thing is surrounded by a chain-link fence. A coil of thick hose hangs from a hook near the front door.

The man gets me out of the crate—on a leash, of course—and takes me straight past the gates through the front door into a small room with a high counter on one side and a steel door with a little window straight ahead.

Whoa. Scent overload—dogs, cats, and even, I think, rabbits.

A stocky middle-aged woman with spiky white hair looks up from a desk, then comes and peers down at me from the counter.

"Got a new one here," the man says. "Bet he won't stay long."

"Oh, a poodle," the woman says. "Pretty boy. But—" she shakes her head. "Can you believe it? Still haven't got the reader back from MicroChip Plus. Or should I call it Micro-Cheap?"

The man smiles at this, but the woman is angry. "I got almost a full house here, and if that SOB boss of mine says I have to put down a dog without checking to see if it has a chip, then I'll quit right now. Hard enough as it is."

The man nods sympathetically. "Ought to make him do it."

She shakes her head. "They should spring for a new one. This is the third time this one's had problems."

"I hear you," the man says, opening the next door and leading me into to a long hall with a cement floor lined with cages on either side. Fluorescent lights set in the center peak of the ceiling run the length of the room. Almost every cage holds a dog, most of whom start to bark when they see me.

Why this is an animal shelter! I was in one once after I ran away from my second boss. Can't say I liked that place much. But Miguel—the one who trained me to be a bed bug dog— took me to his place. Miguel gets most of his dogs from shelters. I wonder if he ever visits this one.

The man puts me in a cage next to a sad looking hound-Lab mix on one side and a bouncy terrier on the other.

He fills a bowl with kibble and another with water. Not as tasty as the food scraps I had earlier, but I have to say that I enjoy it anyway. Doesn't pay to be too picky about food if you're a dog. I exchange sniffs with the hound and the terrier, and then settle down to sleep.

Chapter 14

Animal Shelters

HERE'S THE THING ABOUT SHELTERS. THEY'RE BOR-
ing. All us dogs do is sit in our cages day and night, with
only mealtimes and the occasional visitor to break the monot-
ony. Nothing to do in between except sleep. Like all dogs, I'm
good at sleeping, but even so. A dog can only sleep so much,
and even that's not easy when other dogs—a certain black and
white sheltie and a long-haired Chihuahua mix come to mind—
ward off boredom with constant, high-pitched barking.

I'll admit that I didn't mind so much the first day. Not the
barking, which has been annoying from the start, but the chance
to sleep. I was pretty tired from my long run through the country.
In fact, the pads of my paws were sore and one was a little bloody,
and the cut in my side still ached. Sometimes a full stomach and
a series of good long naps are exactly what a dog needs.

But now, after two long days of rest, I'm energized. And
bored. The main excitement today was when a lanky man with
a wispy beard came and hosed out some of the cages.

Every now and then a visitor comes through the front door,
and all us dogs keep an ear out for that. I hope maybe Miguel
or, even better, Molly or the boss might come through.

So now, when I hear the whine of a car engine, followed by doors shutting and footsteps, I pay attention. Pretty soon, a woman walks in wearing jeans so tight she looks as if she's been poured into them. She clutches the hand of a small child with a jelly-smeared face and grass-stained pants. The woman quickly glances in all the cages.

"Is Maya here?" the child asks in a high voice.

The woman shakes her head and starts to leave just as the white-haired boss comes in. "Y'all see a pit-hound mix in here? Female. Brindle coat?"

The white-haired lady thinks for a second. "We had a female pit mix here last week. When did you lose your dog?"

"She ran off, I dunno, maybe ten days ago."

"Did she have a collar? Microchip?"

"She slipped her collar. We was goin' to get a chip but ain't yet."

"License?"

"We was goin' to get that, too. Been workin' overtime."

The white-haired boss runs a hand through her hair. "We may have had her—like I said, we had a pit mix—but—" she shakes her head, her eyes sad—"she's gone now."

"Gone?" The woman's voice raises several notches in pitch. "Like someone adopted her?"

The white-haired boss shakes her head. "No, I'm afraid she wasn't adopted."

The woman's face darkens. "Y'all killed her?" She glares at the white-haired boss. "Figures." The child begins to cry.

The white-haired boss sighs. "A dog without a collar only has five days here before being put up for adoption. If your pit had had a collar, she would have had ten days. Then we try to find them homes, but we can only keep them an additional three or four days for that." She shakes her head again. "I wish it could be more." She gestures at the cages. "But you can see how full we are and more come in every day."

"Well, thanks for nothing." The woman whirls around, yanks the kid's arm, and walks out so fast the child has to run to keep up.

"Thank *you* for nothing," the white-haired boss says under her breath. Whoa. She's really angry. "Can't be bothered to keep ID on your dog so I had to put that sweet dog down and it's *our* fault? Sometimes I hate this job." Her eyes fill with tears. She strides back out, slamming the door behind her.

Too much emotion. I have to bark, and my barks are joined by most of the other dogs. I keep barking, letting those full-throated sounds drain all the frustration, loneliness, fear, and boredom of the last few days. We dogs raise quite a resounding noise with our combined voices, until finally the man with the wispy beard flings open the door and stoops in the doorway, watching us.

"Hush, ya'll," he shouts a couple of times. "Hush!" But we ignore him, and finally with a shrug, he retreats, shutting the door.

When at last there's nothing left to bark out of me, I stop and get a big drink, and lie down for a nap. I feel better. Barking helps in that way, although it's not nearly as good as running. A good full-out run can cure almost anything.

And maybe it helped the white-haired boss because the next time she comes in, she's grinning broadly. "Guess who gets to leave this place?" she says, standing in front of my cage. "I just talked to your owner—she's been frantic—and she's sending some friends over to pick you up." She reaches through the cage and pats me softly on the head, clearly delighted. "You lucky dog." She glances at some of the other cages and sighs. "I wish they all could be so lucky."

I wag my tail in response, as happy as she is. She talked to *Molly*? I can't help but bark at that.

So I'm awake when an older couple strolls in, older than the boss, that is, but younger than Marmie and Grandjum. They work their way down the aisle, stopping at each cage to study each dog. The man, lean, with graying hair, a sunburned nose, and wire-framed glasses, sometimes writes in a little notebook that he carries. He's wearing thick-soled sandals with bulky wool socks.

Hey, the woman also has sandals and thick socks. She's wearing a heavy, brightly patterned sweater and has thick-framed plastic glasses. She stops in front of my cage. "Henry, I bet this is him!" She studies me with wide-set friendly gray eyes. I study her back.

"More poodle than labradoodle," Henry says coming over to squint down at me.

As I said, I get that a lot.

The white-haired boss comes through the door. "Hey, Sandi. Henry," she says with a nod. "Sorry. I was on the phone when you came in. Our microchip reader's still broken—the company says it'll be a week." She shakes her head in disbelief. "Like it might not be a matter of life or death for these guys. So if you can squeeze in a few extra dogs? There are a couple who are running out of time."

Sandi says, "Okay. We had a few picked out, but we can take the ones with the least time left. And I'll call my foster people, but I think they're all full up right now." She tilts her head at me. "He's a beaut, isn't he?"

"Yeah," the white-haired boss agrees. "I'm so glad his owner found him."

They all stare at me and I sit and stare back.

"A little reserved, are you?" Sandi asks. "But not fearful. Holding back to study the situation. Just like a poodle."

Not rushing forward into an unknown situation seems more like common sense than any poodle trait. Then again, I have noticed that not every dog seems to have that sense.

Henry shakes the chain-link fence. "Here, boy. Kristin said he's had training." He shakes it again. "Sit."

I sit. To be clear, I prefer to work for a reward. "Do the work, get paid" has been my motto from the get-go, which is why (I think I've mentioned before) I didn't make it as a service dog. But there are some commands that have almost become automatic—I hear the word and my body responds. Can't exactly explain it, but *sit* is one of those that I just kind of do without thinking, like *drop it, leave it,* and *down.*

"Down," the man says. I sink to the ground, and get back up when he tells me to stand. "Speak."

This is not an automatic command, although it's one I know. The boss usually tells me to hush rather than to speak. For some reason, he doesn't care much for barking, and he certainly doesn't understand it. So I hesitate. But the man seems nice enough and maybe he has a treat or two in his pocket, though I don't smell any. I give a single bark.

"Impressive," the man says.

The woman nods. She has short brown hair and her cheeks are sunburned as well as her nose. The rest of her face is tanned brown as a walnut. "Hold tight," she says. "You'll be out of here before long."

They move past my cage stopping in front of some of the other dogs, the man making notes. All of us dogs watch with disappointment when they finish and go back through the doors to the front office.

But hey! They return, accompanied by the thin green-shirt man, all carrying leashes! Green-shirt opens the gate to the cage next to me and takes out the hound-Lab mix, while the white-haired boss opens the cage of a sad-eyed blue tick hound. Henry has a golden Lab from near the end of the row. And then, Sandi is opening *my* gate. I try to stay calm but my tail swooshes with excitement. She fits a collar around my neck and soon we're all going out the door and through the gate to a white van.

Inside are wire crates bolted to the floor just like my crate in the boss's van. And each of us dogs is put inside one of the crates. The humans leave us and go back inside, returning in a bit with (I'm sad to say) the yappy border collie.

The sliding door whines shut and then Henry and Sandi climb into the van. The border collie barks excitedly—no surprise there—but then I join in. Can't help myself. We're leaving the shelter!

We drive for some time down winding roads, but I only get a little nauseated. And then we pull into a broad yard with a single-story log cabin at one end, and a sloping-roofed barn at the other. A chorus of barking greets our arrival. At first I think it all comes from the three dogs that rush out to greet us—two elderly Labs and an energetic Yorkie—but then I realize that a good deal of the sound comes from the barn as well.

The man hops out and hefts open the barn door, while the woman gets a leash and takes out the border collie. She comes back for the hound and then it's my turn. My tail droops when the woman puts me on leash and leads me inside. More cages, some with dogs inside them. The cages run the length of the barn on either side of a wide walkway. Another shelter? I hang back. I'm tired of cages, frankly.

With unusual understanding for a human, she says, "Don't worry. This is only for a little bit. You'll be going home tomorrow." She pats my back and, with a gentle tug of the leash, pulls me inside.

At least, as cages go, this is better than the last. For one thing, it's bigger. And there's not a stale urine smell to the flooring, which has some kind of shredded wood over dirt. Not only does it smell better, it's infinitely softer and warmer than the cement floors of the other shelter. While the air in the barn itself is cooler, it's easy to curl down into the bedding and keep warm.

For another, which I find out later in the day, the kibble here is much tastier. Not as good as Kristin's, but better than the other shelter. Plus, we have a new pee/poop place—always interesting—an area of dirt and weeds on the back side of the barn surrounded by a high chain-link fence. Henry takes me there, unclips the leash, and leaves me long enough to thoroughly sniff out all the interesting scents from the other dogs. On my second visit, the Labs and the Yorkie come over to exchange greetings through the fence. They're calm, happy dogs who don't seem to mind strangers on their property.

Finally, when neither Henry or Sandi are in the barn, they leave a radio on that plays soft music and sometimes has a human voice talking in low, soothing tones. Not sure why I like that, but I do, and not just because the music seems to help the border collie yap less.

So, all in all, this new shelter is a much better place. Still, when I burrow down into the sweet-smelling wood shavings at the end of the day, my nose filled with the scents of new people, new dogs, new surroundings, I wish I were back with Molly and the boss in Arlington. Sure the boss's house is small, and yard even smaller, but somehow I really miss that place. And much more than that, I miss Molly.

Suddenly that longing for Molly, for the boss, for *home,* cannot be contained. I sit up and let out a long, mournful howl. Which might have been a mistake because some of the other dogs respond with howls of their own. And of course I have to answer them. And they have to answer back. Pretty soon we're howling up a storm, almost sounding like a pack of coyotes, except instead of howling at the moon on a frosty night, free to roam at will, we're stuck in our cages.

The side door opens and yellow light floods the barn. "Hey guys, take it easy," Henry grumbles. "It'll get better for y'all. I promise. Go to sleep."

And then it's dark again, and we all curl down into our bedding for the night.

Chapter 15

Reunion

THE NEXT MORNING, WHEN SANDI AND HENRY OPEN the barn door, the sun angles in, brightly highlighting a whole world of dust flecks. It's a mild day, and they both wear flannel shirts instead of jackets, although Henry has on boots instead of his sandals.

I have a great time when Henry puts me out in the pee pen. I race around it as fast as I can go in one direction, then turn and go the opposite until finally my legs begin to tire and I start to get a little dizzy. It's a little small to run in, but I excel at sharp turns. And it feels good to be panting from exercise rather than from worry.

Henry watches me. "You are a card," he says, another one of those mysterious phrases since I don't in any way resemble a card.

Just as he's latching the gate after putting me back in my cage, Sandi hurries up to him, waving a newspaper.

"Look at this," she says in a worried voice.

Henry gives her a slight smile and a puzzled look. "What?"

She folds back the paper, pushing it almost into Henry's face. "This." She jabs a finger at a spot in the paper.

Henry squints at it, adjusting his glasses. "Lost," he reads. "Black labradoodle answering to Doodle."

At the sound of my name, I wag my tail. Sandi notices it and frowns.

"Last seen on the Blue Ridge Parkway near Laurel Woods, Virginia. Microchipped. Very friendly. Well-trained. $500 Reward. No questions asked. Please contact Josh Hunter at—"

Hey. That's the boss! The sound of his name sends my tail into action again. Sandi's frown deepens.

Henry reads a number and then takes the paper and holds it up against my crate. "Sure look alike, don't they." He hands it back to his wife.

"Doodle!" she says softly, her eyes intent on me. Haven't heard my name in some time and somehow a bark just erupts from my throat.

And now Henry frowns. Not sure what's going on here. "Where'd Kristin say she got him?"

"From Billy's Pet Supplies just outside of Sparta."

His lips tighten. "Billy Lee Crawford?" He gives me a morose look. "Could be anybody's dog."

Sandi has her phone out, punching buttons. "Kristin will be devastated if…" she hesitates, finger over her phone, "but we have to check." And then, I hear something so unexpected that once again I just have to bark: a voice says "Josh Hunter." But not just a voice. The *boss's* voice.

"Hush," Henry says. Now his expression is as worried as Sandi's. He holds out a hand. "Hush. Sit."

I sit and stop barking. Sandi is saying, "Sandi Bowers from Piney Vale, North Carolina. We run the Crooked Trail Animal

Rescue. Anyway, I saw your ad in the Gazette. We have a dog that fits your description. You said—"

The boss interrupts. "Doodle? You have Doodle?" he shouts. And in the background, I hear a squeal—and an excited voice, *Molly's* voice, asking, "They found Doodle?"

A whole volley of barking pours from me. I leap up and down and then press my nose against the wires of the crate. *Molly!*

I think she hears me, because now she shouts, "Doodle!"

"Hush!" Henry and Sandi command simultaneously, and Sandi starts to move away from my cage. I quit barking so I can hear what everyone is saying.

"Piney Vale?" the boss asks.

"It's a little south of Glade Valley?" When the boss doesn't respond, Sandi adds, "Which is a little south of Sparta?"

"Sparta!" the boss says in amazement. "That's at least an hour from here. Probably an hour and a half. But give us your address and we'll take off right—"

Sandi interrupts. "You say he's microchipped? Because, um, we have a bit of a situation. A friend of ours bought him from a pet shop in Sparta a few days ago—paid a lot of money for him—but he slipped his collar and ran off. She called around and located him at the Piney Vale shelter. We actually picked him up at her request and she's coming over to pick him up at noon, but then I saw your notice in the paper..."

For a moment, the boss doesn't speak, and when he does, he sounds a little scared. "Please keep him until we get there. I have all his records and Molly—my daughter—can bring all sorts of photos. We'll leave this second. We're over in Laurel

Woods, Virginia. I think we can be there before noon, but if not, please, *please* wait."

"We will," Sandi says, her voice reassuring but her face unhappy. "And, we can take him over to Doc Landry's—he has a microchip reader—if ... if we need to."

"Thanks." The boss sounds relieved. And then, "Sparta," as if he can't believe it. "Is he okay?"

"A little dirty, a cut on one ear and a small one on his side, but otherwise looks fine."

They say goodbye, and Sandi shoves her phone in her jacket pocket. "Kristin's not going to be happy," she says.

Henry nods agreement. "But anyone buying a dog from Billy Lee..." He sighs and follows his wife out of the barn.

I pace back and forth as much as the small space will allow, still excited by hearing the voices of Molly and the boss. Eventually, I get tired and lie down by the door, panting despite the cool air. I guess I finally doze off, because I wake up to the sound of voices approaching the barn. Sandi's and Henry's and—uh oh. Kristin's.

"I paid $450 for him. I have a receipt. I don't see how he can be from *Virginia.*"

Henry's voice, low and soothing contrasts with her high-pitched wail. "We just need to let them see him. For their sake as much as yours. If you lost a dog, you'd want to follow up every lead."

"He wouldn't even be *here* if it wasn't for me. I'm the one who called every shelter in three counties 'til I found him. I should have picked him up myself."

Sandi says softly, "But if it were your dog..."

"He *is* my dog." And then, with bluster, "If they say otherwise, they'll have to prove it."

They come into the barn and Kristin rushes over to my cage all gangly arms and legs. "Max! Gosh it's good to see you. You sure scared me. I'll never use that collar again, promise." She waggles her fingers through the bars, but I don't approach her. Her face contorts and she swallows hard.

And then I hear the sound I've been listening for. A car. But not just any car. *The boss's van!*

My barking starts up all the other dogs and once again we're making quite a racket.

"That'll be them," Henry says. "Hey, guys. Hush!" He clips on a leash and lets me out of the cage. "Let's get this figured out. Don't *pull*." I hardly hear him, almost dragging him outside where the boss's van appears at the end of the driveway.

The passenger door opens before the van completely rolls to a stop, and out jumps Molly. "*Doodle!*" she shouts, running towards me.

"Doodle!" Henry also shouts as I bolt forward, tearing the leash from his hands.

And then Molly's arms are around my neck and I'm licking her face (even though I don't usually go in for that sort of thing) and she's kissing me, her eyes wet with tears in spite of a smile so big it looks like it could split her face. "Oh, Doodle," she keeps saying over and over again.

The boss comes up beside her and squats down, and I'm even licking his face, and pushing against him. "Welcome back," he says in a thick voice and—not sure what's going on here—his eyes are wet, too.

We go on like this for a bit, with Sandi and Henry standing off to the side alternately grinning like they've just been fed some really good dog treats and casting worried glances at Kristin, who stands motionless, tears shining in her big round eyes.

And then I see the door Molly left open on the van. I dash over and climb up onto the front seat. I normally ride in my crate behind the front seats, but that door isn't open and I want to make sure when they leave I don't get left behind.

For some reason this makes everyone laugh—well, everyone but Kristin. Molly comes over beside me. "We won't leave you," she says, stroking me under the chin in that way I love. She hugs my neck and I breathe in her scent, my favorite scent in all the world.

The boss pulls out his wallet. "I have his microchip number here if you want—"

Henry shakes his head and shoots a sympathetic look at Kristin. "I think it's pretty clear y'all are his people."

Kristin gives a mute nod, her head down. Molly, watching, pats me on the chest and then goes over to her. "I'm sorry," she says touching Kristin's arm lightly. "You're the one who, um, bought Doodle?"

Another nod, then a pause while Kristin clears her throat. "He—Billy Lee—told me his name was Max. That he'd bought him from the heirs of an old woman who didn't want to keep him after she passed away."

"Quite a story," the boss says fervently. Kristin raises her head sharply. "I meant the pet shop owner's," he adds quickly. "Invented a whole past for him."

The muscles in Kristin's face relax. "I knew Billy Lee can be … unreliable…"

"I'll say. The man's a crook." Henry kicks the gravel with his boot.

Kristin sighs. "Yeah, I've heard stories. But I always wanted a labradoodle, you know? And with things the way they are with Paul—" she glances at Sandi who nods knowingly— "I just thought that Max—er, Doodle—would be perfect."

"I'm sorry," Molly says again.

This makes her eyes water once more and she turns her face toward the barn.

"What stories?" Molly asks, after a brief silence. "Of the pet shop guy."

Henry says, "I've heard he hires people to supply his pet store—from the yards of people who live in neighboring counties. Nothing's ever been proven, though."

Sandi nods in agreement. "Stolen dogs. This isn't the first time a dog he sold ends up belonging to someone else."

"And he doesn't get arrested or anything?" Molly sounds shocked.

"It's one of those things that's hard to prove." Henry continues chipping at the gravel with the toe of his boot.

"Maybe we could figure out how to get him." Molly says. "My mom's a cop."

"In Alexandria," the boss hastens to interject with alarm. "Not in North Carolina."

Molly flushes. "Still, she might know how to contact someone who could check it out. Maybe catch the guy."

No one responds to this and Molly's flush deepens.

The boss turns to Kristin, his eyes sympathetic. "We offered a reward. And we'll pay it to you. At least that won't leave you in the hole."

Kristin gives a little twist of her hand. "You don't have to."

"We want to. We can't thank you enough. We were ... frantic." The boss's voice breaks and he swallows hard.

"Where did he end up?" Molly asks. "We thought we called all the shelters."

"Piney Vale," Henry says.

Molly frowns. "Don't remember that one."

"Good thing I saw the ad," Sandi says.

The boss nods vigorously. "That was Molly's idea. We put ads in every little paper in a radius of—what?"

"Seventy-five miles." Molly relaxes some at the praise in the boss's voice. "Cause we figured someone had picked him up and taken him somewhere."

"Really?" Henry asks, interested. "How was that?"

Sandi interrupts with a gesture that includes the boss and Kristin. "Y'all had lunch? I could make some sandwiches and you could tell us all about it."

Kristin clenches her hands into a fist, her head turning from the boss and Molly back to Sandi. "Um, sure."

The boss's face lights up. "That'd be great. We rushed off without breakfast."

Molly, though, frowns and glances at me in the van.

"Doodle's welcome to join us," Sandi says, noticing. "He's housebroken, right? He seems very well trained."

"When he wants to be," the boss says, sounding more like himself, which is somehow a comfort. He inclines his head toward me. "But, yeah, he's totally housebroken."

Never have quite understood that term. What does peeing outside have to do with breaking houses?

Molly takes off the collar I got from Sandi and snaps on one of my old collars, which frankly smells much better. She clips on the leash and I follow her and the others, including the two Labs and the Yorkie, inside the log home to a big kitchen with big silver appliances and an old wood floor partly covered in oval braided rugs. The Labs sack out on the rugs, while the Yorkie barks at me a few times, until Sandi gives her a look that silences her. Henry asks everyone what they want to drink. Then he fills a coffee cup for the boss and brings two pitchers of tea—sweet and unsweet—for everyone else while Sandi spreads mayonnaise on bread.

Then he joins the others around an old wood table, with a vinyl tablecloth. I've never really liked the scent of vinyl, but I'm happy to lie at Molly's feet, filling my nose with her scent, half-listening, half-dozing as she tells how we got lost together in the woods, and then how she had to go with the paramedics and I stayed behind.

"So what makes you think he was stolen?" Henry gets up and brings plates and forks to the table while Sandi sets down a tray of sandwiches.

"Long story," the boss says, reaching for one as Sandi holds the tray in front of him. "Short version is we found his collar by the parkway and it'd been unclipped, not torn off. And he's never lost his collar before."

"And the long version?" Henry takes a sip of his tea.

The boss holds his cup out toward Molly, who recounts what the cop told them of the turkey-chasing episode. Not exactly accurate, as I wasn't really lost, but this is their version. Humans rarely get things right.

"That cop," the boss says angrily. "Supposed to keep Doodle until animal control arrived and just let him slip through his fingers." He frowns at the tablecloth for a moment. Maybe he doesn't like vinyl either. "Of course Doodle's a damn escape artist when he wants to be."

"Yeah," Kristin agrees quickly.

"So the cop who let Doodle get away—I think he was feeling guilty—got the department to run fingerprints on the ID tag on the collar, and it came up with a guy who's been in jail for meth."

Not sure what meth is, although I think I remember it might be a drug like pot—which I know *very* well from my second boss, the bad one. From the grim expressions around the table, it's not good.

"Wow. Not good." Henry says at last, echoing my thoughts.

"No," the boss agrees. His voice has a husky quality to his voice that I'm not used to hearing. "When we heard that..." he traces a pattern on the tablecloth and clears his throat. "I didn't want to tell Molly, but I thought we'd never see him again."

Molly's eyes widen a little at this. "We were scared," she admits, "but we'd already put the ads in all the papers."

"Molly's idea," the boss repeats with pride.

Molly blushes a little. "But I got the idea from Uncle Armando. When he found out Doodle was missing, he offered to write an ad for the Spanish language paper. And then I thought why not all the papers in the area. So Dad and I got on the Internet and found all the little papers in a hundred mile radius."

"Impressive," Henry says. "And somehow, he ended up at Billy Lee's and that's where you—" he tilts his head at Kristin— "found him."

Kristin nods. "I'd been in several times asking about a labradoodle, so that's why he called me."

"The meth guy probably sold him to Billy Lee," Henry says. "Bottom feeder. He ought to be put out of business."

Everyone agrees.

Molly straightens up in her chair. "I still think we ought to be able to catch him."

"But how'd you get proof?" Sandi asks. She clears away the sandwich tray replacing it with a plate of brownies and everyone reaches for one. "He can always say he doesn't know if a dog is stolen. Especially if it doesn't have a collar."

The boss takes a bite of brownie. "Wonderful!"

"But what if we could make sure he knew a dog was stolen, and then he sells it anyway? To someone else?" Molly asks.

Kristin looks up. "How could we do that?"

Molly starts to explain, and I mean to listen, but frankly it's been a long day, full of excitement, and suddenly my eyes close. The scrape of chairs being pushed back from the table awakens me.

The boss is handing Kristin a check. "No, I insist," he says over her protest.

And then, he hands another to Henry and Sandi. "For your rescue organization. I'm sure countless dogs owe you their lives."

Henry takes it, smiling broadly. "We'll put it to good use."

Molly and Kristin exchange pieces of paper. "Here's my email. I'll call you after I talk to my mom," Molly says. For some reason this makes the boss frown, although Kristin gives the first smile I've seen on her all day.

And then Molly slips me the crust of her sandwich, just like old times, and everyone says goodbye, and the boss puts me in my crate in the van, which is exactly where I want to be.

Chapter 16

Everybody's Talking

NICE PEOPLE," MOLLY SAYS, AS THE ENGINE STARTS and the van rolls down the driveway. She waves at Henry and Sandi who stand with their dogs beside them watching us leave. "How much did you give them?"

"$250," the boss says. "Plus the $500 reward I gave Kristin." He starts tapping the steering wheel. "That'll take a bite out of our savings."

I'm not exactly sure what the boss means except that it's not good. The boss hates biting.

Molly says, "Yeah," in a small voice.

We turn onto the main road, but the boss only drives for a short time before he pulls over to a paved half-circle by the side of the road.

"Oak Ridge Lookout?" Molly asks in surprise.

"Promised Annie I'd let her know about Doodle. Probably won't get another signal till we get home. And—" he gestures beyond the road where the side of the mountain drops off showing a broad expanse of land below—"we'll have a great view."

"Okay. And I'll call Mom. About Billy Lee."

This draws a small sigh from the boss. "Don't forget it's not in her jurisdiction." He gets out of the van, the phone to his ear as soon as he shuts the door.

Molly opens her phone and gives a little gasp of surprise. "Uncle Armando called." She punches a key, and soon I hear his voice. "We got Doodle back!" Molly announces. She tells him the whole story of how I ended up at Henry and Sandi's.

After exclamations of how wonderful it is that I'm safe, Armando tells Molly why he called. Turns out he wants all the family—myself, Grandjum and Marmie included—to come for either lunch or dinner at Dos Amigos before we go back home to Arlington. Molly clearly loves the idea. "That'd be great. I mean, I'll have to ask Dad, but I'm pretty sure he'll say yes."

Next she calls her mother and once again repeats the story of how she and the boss found me. She tells her about Billy Lee, that he cheated Kristin and probably cheats other pet owners, and might be stealing pets.

"I have an idea how we could catch him," Molly says.

"Oh?" Cori's voice takes on a sudden note of caution. "You know how I feel about you—or any layman—getting mixed up with police business."

"I wouldn't be," Molly insists. "But if this guy is running a pet-thief ring—the police could check it out—I know how they could catch him. Doodle could wear a wire."

After a pause, Cori laughs. "That's an original idea."

While I'm trying to puzzle out what Molly means about a wire, Cori says something about having to get a warrant and how the local police might not want the trouble. But, after Molly goes on about how sad Kristin was, and how she and the boss almost didn't get me back at all, she promises she'll check into it.

"Where did you say this Billy Lee works?"

"In Sparta, North Carolina. In Alleghany County."

"Oh." Cori's voice brightens. "I have a friend from police academy who's somewhere in western North Carolina. Luis Gonzales. I'll see if I can find him."

"That'd be great," Molly says just as the boss opens the door and climbs inside. So Molly says goodbye and we're on the road again. I settle down for a nice nap.

The boss's phone wakes me up, with its angry, hornet-like buzz, just as we're turning onto Marmie and Grandjum's road. The boss puts on the brakes as he lifts his phone to his ear.

"Hey, Stu, what's up?"

Stu says something I don't quite understand. Molly leans towards the boss, listening.

"This morning?" the boss says. "At Tri-County General?" He listens some more. "I'm sorry to hear that." After another pause, he says, "Is she up to visitors? We just got back from North Carolina—we found Doodle—yeah, it's wonderful. We could come over right away, if you'd like." Another pause. "Okay, we'll do that. Can Molly come too? Sounds good. I'm ... I'm sorry."

He drops the phone in the cup holder. "Louisa had to be rushed to the hospital early this morning."

The boss just parks the car long enough to let me out and explain the situation to Marmie and Grandjum. Then he and Molly take off again to go to the hospital.

Meanwhile, Bridger and I get reacquainted. He thoroughly sniffs me, taking in all the other dog scents from the shelters.

It's good to be back. Especially since Marmie, who claims I'm too thin, gives us both extra treats.

Molly and the boss come back from the hospital wearing sad faces. Once again, they explain everything to Marmie and Grandjum.

"Stu thinks she'll be able to go home tomorrow," the boss says.

"That's a relief," Marmie says, but her eyes crease with worry.

After that, Molly and the boss spend most of the evening and almost all of the next morning on the phone—Molly talking to her mother; the boss talking to her mother, then agreeing to call her mother's friend, Sergeant Gonzales; the boss rearranging all sorts of bed-bug jobs that had been planned for the coming week; Molly talking to teachers to get her school assignments; and, of course, Molly talking to Tanya and the boss talking to Annie.

When she isn't busy on the phone, Molly sits at her computer working on homework while the boss helps Grandjum replace a part on his truck. All of which for a dog is, in a word, boring. But after all the adventure I've had lately, I find I don't mind boring. I'm happy to lie in the sun with Bridger or at Molly's feet while she works.

Not boring, but disconcerting, is a long argument that the boss and Molly have over the memory card she dropped the afternoon we got lost. Molly wants to try and find it. The boss says it'll be too hard to find and even if they do it'll be "looking for trouble." But, in the end, Molly finally convinces the boss to give it a try—after church on Sunday—with him and Grandjum along to ensure that no one gets lost.

So the next day, after everyone comes home from church, we all go back to the place where we ran into Rocky and Zeke. Well, not all. Marmie stays home, saying the hike "would be death on my poor knees." Bridger gets to come along and he gets to be off-leash, something I can't say. The boss keeps mine on, telling Molly he's not taking a chance of losing me again. Before we leave, Molly puts my working vest on me—the same one I wore at Armando's—and fills the treat bag with chicken treats. I love chicken treats—not quite as good as liver treats, but plenty good enough.

Molly takes the lead—first to the pool, where Bridger and I take the opportunity to get long drinks, and then up and down the hills to the stone outcropping that overlooks the little valley where we saw Zeke.

Along the way, we find the leash that Molly unclipped from me when it got caught in the blackberry vines. The boss frowns as he untangles and pockets it, but doesn't say anything. Everything is pretty much the same as it was the last time I was here, except for some new scents, mostly of the rodent persuasion. The leash keeps me from investigating them as fully as I'd like, and I watch with envy as Bridger follows his nose in wide arcs around us.

When we get to the stone outcropping, Molly points down to the creek below. "That's where they were. And I was here—" She crouches in the shadow of the rock.

"Hey!" She moves down the hill a little and bends down to dig in the leaves under a laurel. When she straightens, she's waving her deer-hunting vest and my scarf. "That's where I hid them," she explains. "So they—the men—wouldn't see us. But then I moved back—" she returns to the rock—"and we heard Rocky, just as I was changing cards. I jumped up and ran." She points in the direction opposite from Marmie and Grandjum's. "And then I kind of got lost. And then Doodle found me later."

Grandjum nods. "Do you think you dropped the card sooner

or later?"

Molly shakes her head. "Not sure, but I think sooner. I wasn't paying attention."

"Okay. " Grandjum sits on a small rock and starts sifting through leaves. "Might as well start looking. But there's a lot of leaves. Could be a needle in a haystack."

I've heard that expression before and know it means something is hard to find, but haven't quite understood it. I mean, needles and hay don't smell at *all* alike, right?

The boss, still peering down at the creek, says, "I'm going to take a look down the hill. See what's there." He hands the leash to Molly, who digs out a small plastic container from her pocket and holds it in front of my nose. I take a deep sniff. It smells mainly of Molly, particularly the oil of her skin, along with faint traces of several plastics. She opens the case and lets me sniff that, too. Same scents. "Here's what we're looking for, Doodle. *Find!*"

Not sure what she wants. Find her? Because she's right in front of me and the container is in her hand. I stand still, looking at her.

"Find!" she repeats.

I don't move.

"Don't think he has a clue," Grandjum says.

True, but I'm pretty sure it's not my fault.

Molly sighs. "Yeah. Maybe it doesn't have a distinctive scent."

It does, but Molly is holding it, which is why I'm confused.

And then Molly says, "I have an idea." She pulls some chicken treats out, which always heightens my interest. "Sit. Stay." She holds out the plastic container again. "Smell."

Hey, we're going to play the Find game. It's a lot like finding bed bugs except in this game Molly hides something and I get a treat for alerting on it. I *love* this game.

"Can you hold him?" she asks Grandjum.

He smiles. "Sure." I sit and stay while she goes behind me, down the slope a little, behind a thick tree trunk. Then she yells, "Find!"

Normally, I race to find the object, but Grandjum has the leash and he doesn't seem to be in a hurry. When we get to Molly, he hands off the leash. I sniff and sniff, and then, as the boss would say, bingo! I dig a little in the leaves, sitting and pointing as I've been taught to do.

"*Good* dog," Molly says, pulling out the little plastic thing. She feeds me several chicken treats. Is this fun or what? We do it again and then again, which is okay by me. Hard to get tired of this game.

Then, Molly says, "Okay, let's move down the trail a bit."

"But I thought you lost it over here," Grandjum says.

"I did, but—I want to try something."

So Grandjum and Molly lead me down the slope, and she has me sit facing away from the top of the hill. She gives me the little container to sniff, which I do to be polite even though by now I know the scent very well. Then, she goes behind me, back up the hill. I want to turn and face her, but I know from long hours with Miguel that I'm not supposed to, so I stay put. Finally, she shouts, "Find!"

"Don't pull." Grandjum gives the leash a little jerk and I ease back. Frankly, he moves too slow for my taste, and I'm relieved when Molly takes the leash again. I cast about, searching for the scent, which is mostly Molly's distinct scent but also the plastic. I try to hone in on the plastic part of it, circling in wide arcs, filling my nose with the scent of leaf mold, dust, damp earth, and, of course, Molly and Grandjum.

But then, I catch the faintest whiff. I stop, sniffing intensely, then walk slowly toward it. Definitely plastic, but not exactly the same. Still, I move closer. I lose it at one point, but circle back and find it again. Closer and closer, and then it's right under my nose, so to speak, sitting half-submerged in the ever-present carpet of leaves. I give the alert.

Molly rushes over and peers at the space around my feet. She brushes away some of the leaves. And then, with a slight gasp, she bends down and delicately lifts up a little plastic container. "Oh my gosh, that's *it*," she cries. "You *did* it! Doodle, you're wonderful!" She holds it up in the air. "He found it, Grandjum! He found it."

I'm still a little confused since I can tell from the scent it's not exactly the same container, but the find seems to be good enough for a treat. Except that Molly's so excited about it that she seems to have forgotten about giving me a treat. I try staring at her. When that doesn't work, I give a single bark.

Molly, never—well, rarely—slow to pick up on things, says, "Oh, Doodle, I'm sorry!" She gives me not just one but half a handful of treats.

And then the boss's head pokes over the ridge. "Did he find it?" he asks with such incredulity that it's almost insulting. He never seems to remember that I always find my bug—or, in this case, little plastic thing.

Molly holds it up in the air, her face suffused in triumph. "I made it a game," she says. "First, I had him look for my other SD card until he got the idea. Then, I didn't hide anything but had him look, and he found this one!"

"Smart girl," the boss says and Grandjum agrees. I think they might be forgetting who did the actual finding here.

We all head back toward Grandjum's while the boss tells us what he found at the base of the hill.

"Whatever they were doing, it wasn't meth," he says with some relief. "We'd be able to smell that a half-mile off, I think. But there was definitely a fire and a lot of cooking. My guess is moonshine."

Grandjum stops a second and leans on his walking stick as if he's glad for a chance to rest. "Bet you're right. Pretty common 'round here. Folks like to make their own. And it's not illegal unless they sell it."

Make their own *moonshine*? I'm totally lost here. I'm not up on all this science stuff like Molly (she studies it at her school), but I've always had the impression the moon's pretty far away and it can only shine at night. And then only on some nights.

Molly, ten steps ahead, gives him an impatient glance. "But Zeke preaches against alcohol. Right? Lizzie said her dad gave up drinking when he joined Zeke's church."

"That's right," the boss agrees.

"So, if my photos come out, I could prove Zeke's a liar."

When we get to Marmie's driveway, Molly asks if she can go on ahead. She takes the leash and breaks out into a run, not stopping until we thump onto the porch. Breathing hard, she goes straight inside, unclips my leash, and rushes to her room, shouting, "Found it!" to Marmie along the way. She inserts the little card that I found into her computer mumbling "Don't be wrecked. Don't be wrecked" as she watches the screen anxiously. She clicks a few times, and then says, "*Yes!*"

Pretty soon she's running back and forth from her computer

to Marmie's printer, only stopping when she has a handful of pages which she shows to the boss and Grandjum and Marmie.

They pass them around with soft exclamations of alarm.

"Zeke's a liar," Marmie says finally.

"That's what Lizzie has been saying all along," Molly says. "We need to show this to Mr. Combs."

The boss, his eyes still on one of the photos, nods slowly. "Can't do it tomorrow as we'll be in Sparta all day." He gives Molly an odd look as if this is her doing. "But I guess we'd have time on Tuesday before we go to Dos Amigos. It's looking for trouble. But for Louisa's sake ... and Nettie's ..."

Molly flashes him a grateful glance. "Let's see Mr. Almighty Zeke deny it all now."

Chapter 17

Undercover

MOLLY WRAPS HER ARMS AROUND MY NECK IN A tight hug. "Don't worry," she whispers in my ear. "It won't be for long."

Her voice is loud and not just because she's close to my ears. It's coming through a speaker in the front of the police van we're in. We're parked on a side street a few blocks away from Billy Crawford's pet store.

"That worked," the boss says. He wears an anxious expression despite repeated assurances that I won't be in any danger. These come from Sergeant Gonzales, a thin, intense man who is in charge of the operation. He keeps telling the boss not to worry. "I've got two detectives watching the back and one in the front, and we'll be listening to every move Crawford makes through Doodle."

He grins down at Molly. "I've worn wires myself and supervised lots of detectives wearing wires, but never wired a dog before."

A wire turns out to be a small little thing that they attached to my chest, hiding it under my fur.

I liked Gonzales the moment I met him and not just because he happened to have treats in his pocket. Earlier, Molly called Tanya and told her how Gonzales has been a friend of her mother's for years. They were both in cop school at the same time, and he ended up in Alleghany County. Evidently, he's a dog lover who jumped at the chance to put Billy Lee Crawford out of business.

"Okay. Party time," Gonzales says, taking my leash.

He's wearing ragged jeans and a stained shirt and shoes splitting out at the side, and has smeared dirt on his face. He looks like some of the homeless people we sometimes see in Arlington, but this is all a disguise. He's undercover, a term that confused me the first time I heard it, but that I now know has nothing to do with blankets and everything to do with pretending to be someone you're not. Molly tells me I'm undercover, too, because I'm wearing the wire. That's a little confusing to me, but I'm happy to go with the flow.

"Okay," he says. We take off down the street, past a fragrant coffee shop, a gas station, and then a bunch of other little stores, until we come to the front doors of Billy's Pet Supplies.

The bell jingles as we walk inside. Gonzales gives a shifty look behind him, as if he's worried about being followed, then brings me over to where Billy Lee stands behind a counter, staring at his laptop.

"Hey." Gonzales casts another furtive glance toward the door. "Found thees dog. Think he might be worth sometin'." He suddenly has a strong Spanish accent. "You geeve me sometin' for him?" He scratches his arms and clears his throat.

A flash of recognition passes over Billy Lee's face as he looks down at me. Then his eyes narrow with suspicion. "Where you'd find him?" he asks.

"Over in Virginia. Near Independence. Running along the side of the road. No collar or nothing."

Billy Lee scratches at the stubble on his chin. "How much you askin'?"

"Fifty. He worth way more than that."

Billy Lee laughs, although his eyes don't change expression. "Think I'm made of money? I might could give you twenty-five. Cain't go higher 'n that."

Gonzales shifts his weight from one foot to the other, scratches an arm, and frowns as if considering the offer. Finally, he reluctantly nods and holds out a hand. Billy Lee opens the cash register and holds out two bills, which Gonzales snatches and stuffs into the pocket of his jeans. He drops the leash and hurries out the front door without a backward glance. Before the door jingles closed, Billy Lee is leading me to a back room where he has a crate that fortunately is a little bigger than the cage I was in last time. "Welcome back," he says in a low, amused voice.

He has his phone out as soon as he latches the gate.

A woman's voice says, "Kathy."

"Hey, Kathy. Billy Lee here. I know how disappointed you was the other day when you came in looking for a labradoodle. And so I did some calling around and I managed to find another one if y'all are interested. He's got a great personality, will make someone a great dog."

"Oh," Kathy sounds excited. "Yes. I'm definitely interested. What color?"

"Black. Weighs about 75 pounds."

"Hmm." Her enthusiasm deflates. "I was kind of hoping for a golden one."

"Well, suit yerself. But doodles are hard to find these days and this dog is a particularly fine one."

"How much are you asking?"

"Well, normally I'd git $500—he's got the breeding and training to make it worthwhile and that's what one of them doodle rescue groups would charge. Or even more. But I'll give him to you for $300 if you can get him today. I got several other dogs coming in and no space to put 'em. Cash only."

This seems to intrigue her. "Okay," she says. "I'll come by and look at him."

Just as he's folding his phone, the bell on the door tinkles. He hurries out to the front, leaving me in my cage.

"Hey, Billy Lee," says a woman's voice. Why, it's Kristin! She sounds dejected and talks more slowly than normal. "Max is gone. I think maybe someone took him from our yard. Either that or he jumped the fence. And I had an appointment to get him microchipped the next day. You know about anyone finding a lost labradoodle?"

"Cain't say I have," Billy Lee says. "But I'll keep my ear out. Sorry to hear that. Tough luck."

"Could—would you let me put up these posters? In case anyone coming in has seen him?"

"Sure thing. Give 'em to me and I'll put them up for you. And I'll tell the folks on my listserve to let me know if anyone finds a dog of that description."

"Thanks." Her voice breaks. "I only had him for a few days, but now he's like family, you know?"

"Yeah," agrees Billy Lee, his voice full of sympathy. "Don't you worry. I'll spread the word best I can."

"Okay," Kristin says in a small voice. "Thanks so much!"

The bells tinkles again as she leaves. Billy Lee stays up front. I don't know how long of a nap I take, but awake to Billy Lee's voice. "Hey, Kathy. He's in the back room. I'll git him."

He leads me out front over to an attractive plump woman, neatly dressed in a pantsuit, who takes the leash eagerly. She smells of cinnamon and bread, and she leans over me with an engaging smile.

"Well, bless your heart, aren't you beautiful!" she says in a warm voice. Something about her makes me wag my tail.

"And friendly, too." She strokes my back and under my chin, and then straightens up. "Okay. I'll take him. What's his name?"

Billy Lee's eyes light up. "The guy I got him from says his name was Ringo, but you can name him anything. They's smart, these labradoodles."

"Hey, Ringo," the woman coos as she opens her purse and pulls out some bills. "I'll need a receipt—a bill of sale?"

Billy Lee frowns. "I don't do no returns. Hard enough to stay in business as it is."

"I understand, but my husband insists on a receipt for everything. Especially this much money." She rolls her eyes, like she thinks her husband is crazy. Billy Lee sighs, his eyes on the money she's holding.

"Guess I could do that." He digs around behind the cash register for a piece of paper, then starts writing on it.

"Wonderful!" She gives him a big smile, counts out the money and exchanges it for the paper, which she pockets. "You've made my day! Thanks so much!" She waves at Billy Lee as she leads me out of the store.

Hey! I lift my nose, then see what I'm smelling. Molly and the boss stand beside the police van which is now just a few cars down from the pet shop.

Molly runs up to me and takes the leash. "Doodle, you did great! Perfect! We heard it all!"

The boss joins her. "Good dog," he says with enthusiasm.

Kathy turns, joined by Gonzales, and marches back into the pet shop. They reemerge shortly with a handcuffed, scowling Billy Lee between them. Gonzales shoves him in the back of a police car. "See you at the station." He and Kathy wave as the car pulls away, big grins on both their faces. Then they come over to where Molly and the boss and I are standing.

"Slam dunk," Gonzales says happily. "What a great idea to wire him. Speaking of which, I guess we'd better get it off." He leans over and pulls off the little thing stuck to my chest. "I think your daughter and your dog could have a career in law enforcement." He gives me a few pats. "Would you like to be a police dog, Doodle?"

Not sure what he means, since everyone knows that German shepherds are the ones who go into police work. A little too intense for my taste, but in my experience German shepherds are all about intensity.

And then Kathy joins in. "Oh, Doodle, you were just perfect!" She reaches into her pocket. "From one undercover agent to another." She hands me a few very tasty treats. Kathy was undercover? Who knew? Certainly not me, and I'm guessing not Billy Lee Crawford either.

I may not be cut out for police work, but if these are the kinds of treats I'm going to get, I'm thinking undercover might be the way to go.

Chapter 18

Looking for Forgiveness

THE NEXT MORNING, EVERYONE'S UP EARLY. MOLLY and the boss pack and load their suitcases into the van. We're going home today, but not before we do a couple of things. First, according to Molly, we'll visit Lizzie. Then, we'll go to a celebration lunch at Los Dos Amigos.

"Zeke's here," Molly says when we pull up in front of Lizzie's house. She points to his truck parked by the barn. She twists her hair and I can smell the tension—almost fear—pouring from both her and the boss.

I stare at the truck and sniff. No sign or scent of Rocky, which I consider a good thing.

The boss has hardly turned off the engine before both Zeke and Will come striding over, neither of them looking friendly.

The boss gets out and opens the sliding door to the van, but leaves me in my crate. Molly, clutching her stack of printed photos under one arm, says, "Can I have Doodle beside me?" She gives the boss an anxious glance. "It ... helps to have him close."

The boss studies her, then glances over at Zeke and his pickup. "I guess since Rocky isn't here..." He gets my leash and lets me out. Molly stands nervously beside him, one hand holding the photos, the other my leash.

"Hey, Josh." Will's voice is strained and cold. I hear a click of a latch and then a creak. The front door of the house opens and Lizzie and Nettie stand behind the screen, watching. Molly lifts the leash hand in a small wave to Lizzie. Will gives them a quick glance, his lips tightening, then turns back to the boss. "I do believe I made it clear last time that I didn't want you on my property."

"Abundantly clear," Zeke agrees, his eyes brimming with hostility.

The hair rises on my back.

"It's not a social visit." Josh's voice is every bit as cold and tense as Will's. "Molly here has something to show you."

Her eyes fixed on Will, almost as if she's afraid to look at Zeke, Molly holds out a couple of the pages, which shake a little in her hand. "These are photos I took before I got lost. Before Rocky chased us off." Now she turns to look Zeke in the face. "Just a ways up from Sycamore Hollow, where you told Lizzie the land belonged to your cousin."

Zeke's lips curl into a smile, but his eyes flash with anger. I suppress a growl. "No idea what you're talking about."

"Really?" the boss says. "Then maybe you have a twin? Because this man looks *exactly* like you." He jabs a finger at one of the photos that Will holds.

Will frowns at the photos, then looks up at Zeke with a puzzled expression.

"Here are a few more," Molly says.

Will takes the photos she holds out and shuffles through them, his face darkening.

The boss, watching him, says "It doesn't come down to Zeke's word against Molly's and Lizzie's anymore. She has the photos to prove her point." He turns to Zeke. "But neither of us likes you calling Molly a liar."

"And even worse"—now the chill in the boss's voice turns to anger—"even worse, when Molly was missing, you were there on the scene. And you didn't come forward. All those dedicated people searching most of the night in the wrong places because you didn't come forward. When a child's life was on the line."

"That's not true," Zeke says. "She wasn't there, just the dog." And then he clamps his mouth shut. The glare he shoots at Molly makes me growl. The boss hears it and looks down at me, but for once doesn't tell me to hush.

Will, who has been so still as to be frozen, sorts through the photos a second time, his expression unreadable. And then he looks through them a third.

"That's a moonshine still," the boss says. "And that's your Man of God there, drinking from a quart jar."

"I don't have to listen to this," Zeke says. "God is my witness and He knows I've been a righteous servant." He turns to Will. "This is a test of your faith—not just your faith but your faithfulness. Don't listen to them."

Molly's hand trembles on my neck. She takes a deep breath. "So, I guess lying is righteous? You preach about not drinking, then you do it yourself?"

Zeke gives her a look of pure hatred. I growl again and move forward a little, but Molly tightens the leash and the boss says softly, "Doodle, *no.*"

"That's it." Zeke peers down his nose at Will, his head held high. "I will not stay in the presence of those who are too blind to see the truth." He turns and strides to his pickup, slamming the door as he gets in. He wheels the truck around with a squeal of brakes, and then roars down the road in a cloud of dust.

"Can't say I'll miss him," the boss says under his breath.

Will stands like a statue, holding the photos in his hand, not meeting the boss's eyes.

No one speaks until the sound of Zeke's truck has faded entirely.

"Will," the boss says in a tone so full of pain that I look up at him in alarm. "I can't say I know what it's like to lose a child. But when Molly um ... disappeared, I thought if something had happened to her, if I didn't ... get her back ... I thought ... I might die. Or want to." Whoa. The boss's eyes well with tears.

Will nods, and his eyes are wet as well.

"I can only imagine how you've suffered after Adam's death. But I don't understand why you'd listen to a man like Zeke. What could he give you that would be worth cutting yourself off from family?"

Now the tears run down Will's cheek. "Forgiveness," he says in a husky voice. "He made me feel Adam's death wasn't my fault."

The boss stares at him a second. Molly grips the fur on my neck and flashes a glance at Lizzie, still standing in the doorway.

"It was an *accident.* You don't need someone like Zeke to tell you that. Anyone who says different, religious or not, is an idiot. You will never see your son again because of an *accident.* Not anything you did.

"But what you *have* done is separate Louisa and Stu from their daughter and grandkids, so that for them Nettie and Lizzie might as well be dead. And that's not accidental. That's *your* doing. The loss you feel over Adam—that's what Louisa feels. She's dying and she can't see her daughter and grandkids—because somehow Stu and Louisa *don't agree with you?* So *what?*" The boss's voice breaks and he clears his throat. "Even if Louisa were in perfect health, it's wrong to keep her from her family. It's stupid and small-minded. No, not just stupid and small-minded. Mean. It's mean, Will."

Will doesn't move, his eyes unfocused, as if looking inward.

The boss shakes his head. "Louisa doesn't have long. Did you know she went into the hospital yesterday?"

From the doorway, I hear Nettie gasp. She leans against the screen, rigid, her eyes fixed on her husband.

"She's home now, but who knows for how long. And Nettie's missing time with her mother that she'll never—never, ever—have again."

The boss swallows and for a few moments no one speaks. Finally, he sighs. "Adam's death was a terrible tragedy. But if it gives us any meaning at all, it's that life is fragile and can be gone in a second. So we damn well better make the most of the time we have with those we love—hold them close and make every moment count. Nettie can't do that with her mother—because of you."

Will stands as if frozen, no sign of response on his face.

After a moment, the boss grimaces and turns to Molly. "Let's go. I've said all I have to say." He stalks back to the van without a backward glance.

We drive away in silence, leaving Will still motionless in his yard.

Chapter 19

Los Dos Amigos

AFTER WE LEAVE LIZZIE'S PLACE, WE GO BACK TO
Marmie and Grandjum's. The boss calls Stu and has a
long conversation with him, then walks through the house,
looking for anything he might have forgotten to pack.

Then we're back in the van on our way to the restaurant.
Marmie and Grandjum leave a little before us in their own car
because the boss says we'll be going straight home after lunch.

Armando opens the door to greet us when we arrive and
ushers us to a side room where a long table has been set up.
The place smells as wonderful as ever. Grandjum and Marmie,
already seated, nod at us as we come in. They're talking to
a strong featured, elegantly dressed woman with silver hair
swept back into a thick bun. I've never seen her before, but I
see Kristin's here, sitting next to Kathy, her face animated and
her big hands darting one way and then another as she speaks.

And then, in walk Henry and Sandi, who wave at Kristin
and Kathy and then head over to me.

"How's our favorite undercover labradoodle?" Sandi pulls
out a handful of treats and gives them to me.

At the moment, never better.

Armando takes Molly's hand and leads her over to the silver-haired woman beside Marmie. "Mariela, can you believe how our little Maria has grown? Only we're to call her Molly now." He lifts his eyebrows slightly at this.

Mariela rises out of her chair and takes Molly's hand in both of hers. "Oh, oh, oh," she coos softly. "Molly! I can't tell you how happy it makes me to see you! What a beautiful girl you've become."

Molly's face glows and her hand moves to her throat.

Mariela, noticing, says, "That's a beautiful necklace."

"My mother gave it to me," Molly says with pride.

"Of course. *La mariposa.*" Mariela has a deep, warm laugh. "Your grandfather used to call your mother his little *mariposa,* but I guess you already know that."

Molly nods. "She told me when she gave it to me. But I didn't know about the fight they had. Not until Uncle Armando told me."

Armando winks at Molly. "Ah, but I have good news about that, thanks to you. Cori called her mother last week. And—" Armando pauses before saying with a flourish of his hand— "she talked to her father as well."

"For the first time since she ran away," Mariela adds.

Molly's face splits into a wide grin. "I told her what you said about her father—how much he missed her, but ... I didn't think she'd listen."

"I'm sorry she couldn't be here," Mariela says. "It would have been wonderful to see her."

"She's always really busy. She's a detective and she's on a new case." Molly steals a glance at the door as she says this, as if looking for someone. But she just said her mother wasn't going to be here, right? That's who she's usually looking for. And usually disappointed, I might add.

Kathy tilts her glass at Molly. "Speaking of detectives, Sergeant Gonzales asked me to tell you how sorry he is that he can't be here. Had a homicide over near Stratford. But he said to tell you that catching Billy Lee Crawford was the most fun he's had in ages, and any time y'all—" she gestures to Kristin and Molly, and then down to me—"want to run another sting, count him in."

Huh? I don't remember anyone actually being stung.

The boss and I take a seat—me on the floor, of course—near the end of the table. I prefer to sit with Molly, as the boss never slips me bites of food, but she's still talking to Mariela. A waiter delivers baskets of chips and bowls of salsa to the table, and soon everyone's crunching them down.

"So, Molly," Armando dabs at his moustache with his napkin, "tell us about this great 'sting'. I have heard via *La Habladera* that pets are safer because of you?"

Molly flushes. "Kristin and Officer Wells—"

Kathy waves a chip in protest—"Call me Kathy."

"Kristin and, um, Kathy both helped, too. And Doodle!"

I wag my tail. Whoa. Now the *boss* hands me a treat. I'd smelled them in his jacket pocket, of course, but didn't expect to get one. Not unless there were bed bugs to find.

Molly launches into the story of how Billy Lee bought me from Sergeant Gonzales and then sold me to Kathy even though he'd promised to help Kristin find me.

"You were so good," Molly says to Kristin. "Totally convincing."

A fleeting expression of sadness crosses Kristin's face. "Well, it wasn't all an act. I really was sorry to lose Doodle." Then she brightens. "But—I have good news. Thanks to Henry and Sandi." She casts a grateful glance in their direction. "I've adopted Lucy, one of their rescue dogs—a hound/Labrador mix."

Hey, I think I remember her. Very sedate dog. She might help Kristin relax some.

"She's a great dog—calm, loving. Hard to believe no one came to find her," Sandi says.

"But they've had her for over a month, and run ads in the paper and no one has claimed her," Kristin hastens to add. "And she's not microchipped." She takes a bite of chip and swallows it. "I really thought I wanted a labradoodle," she says, looking at me, "partly to please my husband because they don't shed, but, um, that may not be relevant anymore." She and Sandi exchange a glance. "And Sandi convinced me that tempera-ment is more important than looks or whether or not a dog sheds, and Lucy has a wonderful temperament."

When Kristin takes another bite of chip, Armando says, "But we were talking about the great sting. So Kristin pretended she'd lost Doodle." He frowns slightly at Molly. "And you said she was great. Were you in the store with her?"

Molly explains how she and the boss and Sergeant Gonzales heard it all because Doodle was wearing a wire.

"That's one for the record books," Kathy says. "At least in our neck of the woods. A dog wearing a wire. We couldn't have done it without a warrant, but fortunately the local judge is a dog lover. And, of course, we had enough evidence to justify it." She grins.

"Those posters I gave him?" Kristin jabs a chip into the air indignantly. "Went right into the trash! He lied straight to my face."

"Bottom feeder," Henry says.

Kathy says, "Well, he's scum all right, but he just sold the pets. The really good news is that he gave up three guys who did the stealing."

"I wonder if one of them was the man who took Doodle," the boss says.

Kathy shakes her head. "None of them have admitted it so far. But one, Larry Ketchum, was a meth-head so it might have been him."

Molly steals another glance at the door, and then the boss does the same thing. No idea why.

The waiters enter, their arms sagging under heavy trays. They pass plates filled with fragrant dishes to those seated around the table. Molly takes a seat between Armando and Mariela, and soon everyone's eating and talking among themselves.

Just before I settle down for a nap—don't think the boss plans to dole out any more treats—I hear Marmie and Grand-jum laugh out loud as Armando, hands flying in elaborate gestures, finishes a story. Mariela listens with an indulgent smile on her face. And Molly—who has always longed for family the way a dog longs to be part of a pack—Molly has never looked happier. I catch the boss watching her, an expression of contentment on his face that I rarely see.

I close my eyes, awakening when the conversation suddenly stops and the boss stiffens and turns toward the door. I follow his gaze. Why, Stu's here, his eyes blinking behind his thick lenses, his chipmunk cheeks bright as ever. And—I hear Molly gasp—Lizzie's beside him.

"Lizzie!" Molly leaps from her chair and runs to hug her friend.

The boss is on his feet as well, crossing over to Stu and embracing him. "Good to see you here. And *wonderful* to see—" He tilts his head at Molly and Lizzie who are talking in soft but excited tones.

"Yes, wonderful," Stu agrees, his eyes on Molly and Lizzie as well. "Sorry we're a little late. Louisa sends her greetings to everyone. She would have loved to be here, but she's not up to it." His lips tighten for a moment, but then relax into a smile. "Instead, she's visiting with Nettie and Becca. They came over not long after your visit. For the first time in over a year."

He claps an arm on the boss's shoulder. "We have you to thank for that. Nettie told us how you laid it on the line to Will."

The boss shakes his head. "It wasn't me. Molly had the photos that showed him what an a—" he stops himself—"a jerk Zeke really is."

"Well, in Nettie's words, 'you preached him a fine sermon.'"

The boss shifts his weight, looking profoundly uncomfortable. "Just trying to be honest. As a friend." Neither of them say anything for a moment. "So you told Will he and his family were invited?"

Stu rubs the bridge of his nose. "Yeah. And he agreed to let Lizzie come. I told him he was invited too, but ... well ... I think it's just too soon after everything that's gone on."

The boss nods. "I didn't expect him. But, well, I hoped."

But—" Stu straightens his glasses. "Nettie said that it wasn't the still or the drinking that made Will change his mind about Zeke. It was that Zeke didn't help you when Molly was missing."

"Pretty unforgiveable," the boss agrees. "I get angry just thinking about it. But at least Will knows what kind of man Zeke really is."

"At least I get to see my daughter and grandkids again," Stu says. "That's all I care about." Whoa. Suddenly tears are running down his cheek. He swallows hard.

The boss lays a hand on Stu's shoulder for a moment, and then motions to the empty chair beside him. "Let's get you some food."

Armando signals a waiter to bring extra plates and silverware, and scoots his chair over to fit Lizzie in beside Molly. And once again everyone's eating and talking and laughing.

Finally, the boss pushes back his chair. "We really have to go." He checks his phone. "Molly has school, I have work. And—" he pulls out his phone and checks it briefly—"I think it's late enough we'll miss the brunt of traffic."

The boss worrying about traffic? Everything's back to normal! He stands up. "Ready to go home, Doodle?"

Do dogs bark? I jump up and lead the way to the van, and for once the boss doesn't tell me not to pull.

Acknowledgements

I'M DEEPLY GRATEFUL TO EXPERTS WHO GENEROUSLY give of their time to help authors get things right.

Erik Bullinger, EMS Captain of the Burlington Fire Department, in Burlington, Iowa, answered a host of questions about the on-site procedures and priorities for an EMS rescue, and helped me find a realistic path through a critical juncture in the story.

Paula Xan McCollum at Precision K9, LLC, in Boise, Idaho, answered questions related to search and rescue teams.

A visit to Veronica A. Bryant, Animal Control Officer at the City of Galax Animal Control Center, helped me understand the hazards, both physical and emotional, that her job presents on a daily basis. Not only is she responsible for the strays picked up and brought to the shelter, she also works to document and prosecute cases of animal cruelty. After hearing her speak with compassion, eloquence, and sorrow about pets who end up at the shelter, often without any kind of identification, I rushed home to double-check that all the contact information listed on my dog's license and microchip were up to date. Too many people who love their dogs and otherwise treat them well, don't keep current ID tags on them. A dog who ends up in a shelter without a collar or microchip has half the allotted time as a dog who has ID, and a very slim chance of survival.

Betty Sutton gave me insight into the various ways that members of the Twin County Humane Society work with local shelters to foster and find new homes for adoptable strays. Many a dog, whose time at a shelter has run out, has been given a reprieve and eventually a new family through the efforts of these hard-working animal lovers.

As in previous books, I owe a debt to Marti Jones. My interviews with her when she was the Executive Director and Senior Staff Attorney at the Immigration Project in Bloomington, Illinois, helped me to create the histories of Cori's family and extended relatives.

Naturally, any errors in my depiction of EMTs, rescue personnel, animal shelters, or the Mexican-American immigration experience are my own.

I'm immensely grateful to first readers Sara Hoskinson Frommer and Virginia Smith, experts in their own right, for reading the manuscript and offering insight and encouragement. Thanks also to Ardis Kenney for applying her copy editor's eagle eye to the book.

I owe a debt of gratitude to M. Shayne Bell and to Lee Allred, both fine writers themselves, for their support and encouragement over the years. Kristine Kathryn Rusch and Dean Wesley Smith have helped me and countless writers in ways too numerous to list here.

Thanks as always to my son Joseph Kroupa, my go-to Photoshop and design guru and all-round technical advisor.

And finally, thanks to my husband Tom, who not only makes it all possible but worthwhile.

About the Author

SUSAN J. KROUPA IS A DOG LOVER WHO ADOPTED Shadow, the obedience-impaired labradoodle whose antics served as the inspiration for Doodle. (Read about the adventures and misadventures of raising Shadow at doodlewhacked.com.)

She is also an award-winning author whose fiction has appeared in *Realms of Fantasy*, and in a variety of professional anthologies, including *Bruce Coville's Shapeshifters*.

Her nonfiction publications include features about environmental issues and Hopi Indian culture for *The Arizona Republic*, *High Country News*, and *American Forests*.

She lives in the Blue Ridge Mountains in Southwestern Virginia, where she's busy writing the next Doodle-bugged mystery. Visit her online at susankroupa.com.

The Doodlebugged Mysteries

Bed-Bugged: *Doodlebugged Mysteries #1*

Ask Doodle why he flunked out of service-dog school and he'll tell you: smart and obedient don't always go hand in hand. Now he has a new job sniffing out bed bugs for his new boss, Josh Hunter. The best part of the job? Molly, the boss's ten-year old daughter, who slips Doodle extra treats when she's not busy snapping photos with her new camera. But Molly has secrets of her own. And when she enlists Doodle's help to solve a crime, his nose and her camera lead them straight to danger. A charming mystery for dog lovers of all ages.

Out-Sniffed: *Doodlebugged Mysteries #2*

Doodle's nose gets put to the test when Molly starts training him to find something very different from bed bugs to clear her best friend's brother from drug charges. But when Doodle fails to find two vials containing bed bugs during a practice for an important certification trial, the boss is furious.

It takes all of Molly's ingenuity and Doodle's keen intelligence to sniff out the real villains and set things right again.

Nominated for the Maxwell Medallion by the Dog Writers Association of America.

Dog-Nabbed: *Doodlebugged Mysteries #3*

A trip to the Blue Ridge Mountains quickly turns dangerous when Molly tries to help a friend and runs smack into an unscrupulous man with a big secret. And Doodle discovers that while it's no fun being lost in the woods, it can be worse to be found—by the wrong person.

Bad-Mouthed: *Doodlebugged Mysteries #4*

Doodle's the first to admit he doesn't get Christmas. His job is to find bedbugs for his boss's bedbug detection business and to watch over the boss's ten-year-old daughter, Molly. It is not to play a black sheep in a Christmas pageant, a lose-lose situation for sure. Not to mention that just when things start to get interesting, Doodle attracts the attention of a popular videoblogger, whose subsequent "feature" jeopardizes the boss's business.

Throw in a handful of threatening letters, a devastating fire and some lost dogs, and Molly and Doodle have their hands—well, in Doodle's case, his paws—full finding out just who's been naughty and who's been nice.

Ruff-Housed: *Doodlebugged Mysteries #5*

Sit. Stay. Be polite with strangers. What could be easier?

That's what Doodle thinks when Molly signs him up to take the Canine Good Citizen Test at the annual DogDays Fair.

But the test turns out to be no walk (or sit) in the park. Did he miss the memo about the explosions?

While Molly and her friends investigate, a dog disappears, with repercussions that threaten the bonds of an entire family.

Throw in a bullying neighbor and a chase across a squirrel-infested park near the White House, and Doodle begins to wonder if he and Molly have bitten off more than they can chew.

Winner of the 2017 Dog Writers Association of America AKC S.T.A.R. Puppy and Canine Good Citizen Award for the best writing about the AKC Canine Good Citizen Program.

Mis-Chipped: *Doodlebugged Mysteries #6*

One dog, two microchips, two claims...

When Molly and Doodle watch a good friend's dog race in flyball tournament, Doodle thinks flyball might be fun. Until the dog shows an unusual talent for the sport and someone else claims to be the dog's owner. Thrown into a world of heartless criminals and hard choices, Molly and her friend set out to find the truth. But it takes Doodle's nose, Molly's persistence, and a big dose of courage to set things right.

Visit susankroupa.com to learn more about these and upcoming new titles.

Made in the USA
Middletown, DE
19 August 2020

15683619R00113